I0679240

Sherlock Holmes: Studies In Legacy

Luke Benjamen Kuhns

First edition published in 2013
© Copyright 2013
Luke Kuhns

The right of Luke Kuhns to be identified as the author of this
work has been asserted by him in accordance with the Copyright, Designs and Patents Act 1998.

All rights reserved. No reproduction, copy or transmission of
this publication may be made without express prior written
permission. No paragraph of this publication may be repro-
duced, copied or transmitted except with express prior written
permission or in accordance with the provisions of the Copyright Act 1956 (as amended). Any person who commits any
unauthorised act in relation to this publication may be liable to
criminal prosecution and civil claims for damage.

All characters appearing in this work are fictitious. Any resemblance to real persons, living or dead, is purely coincidental.
The opinions expressed herein are those of the authors and not
of MX Publishing.

Paperback ISBN 9781780924205
ePub ISBN 9781780924212
PDF ISBN 9781780924229

Published in the UK by MX Publishing
335 Princess Park Manor, Royal Drive,
London, N11 3GX

www.mxpublishing.com

Cover design by Phil Dragash
Compiled by www.staunch.com

Dedication

To my Grandfather Robert (Bob) L. Beitler (1931 - 2013)

&

My friend Reverend David Stanley-Burnett Jones (1924 - 2013)

Acknowledgement

I want to thank my God and Saviour, Jesus Christ, from whom comes so much goodness and in whom all my hope is placed; as Sherlock Holmes said, "It is only goodness which gives extras, and so I say again that we have much to hope from." I wish to thank my friends and family who have continually supported and encouraged me in all my writing endeavours. A warm greeting and thank you to you, the reader, for spending your hard earned money on this book; I shake you warmly by the hand and trust you will enjoy it! Thank you to MX Publishing for your support and also to the vast Sherlockian community, which I have become a part of. Thank you to Phil Dragash for the brilliant cover and to Nadine Dare for being my editor! Lastly, before I run out of room, I want to say a very quick "Hello to Jason Isaacs!"

The Untold Adventures of Sherlock Holmes
Volume II

Being a reprint from the reminiscences of
John H Watson MD
late of the Army Medical Department

Contents

Introduction

Tucked away in the vaults of Cox & Co. bank at Charing
Cross rests a worn tin dispatch box bearing the name: John
H. Watson, M.D., late of the Indian Army. This battered
container is one of my greatest treasures, for within it lie
hundreds of case records from my adventures with Mr
Sherlock Holmes.

Having recently received a letter from Holmes, I was
made aware of his concern regarding an old case I had
published. He believed I had told only part of the story.
Writing, as is his habit in these later years, from his home in
Sussex, he remarked:

"I see that you have recently disclosed the events
concerning Her Majesty the Queen during her Diamond
Jubilee. It is only proper to relate what followed, do you not?
The time is ripe for a fuller account, my dear Watson."

After reading his request, I was compelled to revisit our
old records and prepare a complete account of those events
connected to the Jubilee. On a cold and rainy afternoon, I
travelled to the bank at Charing Cross and requested the
dispatch box. With great care, I carried it home and began
my search.

Among the loose papers, I discovered one of my old
red, leather-bound journals, originally acquired from Cox &
Co. of Bond Street. Unravelling the thread that kept it
sealed, I began to read the entries Holmes had urged me to
revisit.

Within this journal, I had recorded a sequence of events
from early 1899—events both grotesque and intellectually
stimulating in equal measure. The year bore a resemblance to
1895, when Holmes was at the height of his powers. Upon

reviewing the material, I realised that I had separated this case from earlier accounts only because its origins dated back to 1897.

These cases began in February of 1899, when a succession of mysteries and murders consumed the daily lives of Holmes and me. A looming presence seemed to haunt us at every turn. I cannot recall a more trying period in our partnership, save for a few exceptional instances.

I must also confess that the delay in publishing these accounts was partly at Holmes's request. He wished the details withheld, as the cases had already stirred considerable attention in the newspapers. Now, with sufficient time having passed, I feel at liberty to present them in full.

Thus, I offer these further untold adventures to the public—an honest and complete account of those strange affairs that were once only partially reported.

—Dr John H. Watson

A Study in Hysteria

Mrs Dabish

"She has been through a strange and grotesque affair," said Holmes sitting comfortably in his chair, smoking a cherrywood pipe. In his hand he held a letter that had come to him earlier that day.

"What affair is this?" I asked.

Holmes extended his arm towards me, the paper dangling between his fingers. I laid down my copy of *The Daily Telegraph* and gripped the paper.

"Would you read it aloud, Watson?"

"Haven't you just read it?"

"I would be most appreciative."

I rolled my eyes. "Very well."

I unfolded the letter. It was handwritten on hotel paper. I read aloud the following:

Mr Holmes,

Re: Mrs Isabelle Dabish of Dulwich, London. I require your urgent assistance.

I have come into the care of a young woman named Isabelle Dabish. She has been through a strange and grotesque affair.

A time ago, her husband, Doctor Walter Dabish, went missing and now is presumed dead.

The event of her husband's disappearance resulted in a strange case of hysteria, to the point of a complete psychological breakdown.

She was found in her home in Dulwich with a self-inflicted knife wound to her chest.

On normal grounds, I would not need the aid of a detective, private or otherwise. However, there is something odd about her.

Pieces that I cannot completely put together, even as a specialist in psychoanalysis.

I have a strong suspicion something is wrong. I believe there is a deeper reason for her mental deterioration. Mr Holmes, I request you come and see me in person to discuss this matter in greater depth.

I am currently staying at the Savoy Hotel while I care for Mrs Dabish.

You will find me there tomorrow from midday. Please come.

Dr Sigmund Freud

"*The* Dr Sigmund Freud!" I said. "That man is a genius. Are you going to meet with him?"

Holmes raised himself from his chair and crossed his arms, his pipe smouldering in his clasped hand. His face tensed as he paced back and forth a few moments.

"Look at his writing, my dear Watson. The letter was written in a hurry. Freud, a liberal man he may be, is still a man who must work with control in his profession, meaning that whatever has happened to this woman, Dabish was it? Yes, Dabish. Whatever has happened to her is shocking enough to unsettle a man who spends his time working with the psychologically shattered individuals."

"Holmes, come now!" said I, "How can you tell his writing is of an unsettled nature?"

"Observation, Watson." He walked over to a desk and pulled out a bundle of letters. "This is not my first letter from the famous Dr. No, I have sent him many letters and received several replies over the years. Though it is unknown to him that I am the one with whom he conferred, as all my letters to Dr Freud were under a pseudonym because I was consulting him over matters relating to the late Professor

Moriarty and his associates, such as Doctor Perny, before his recent and untimely death. Heart failure, the papers report, was the cause. I very much doubt that."

"You stray from the point. Perny is old news. Dr Dabish, I know this man, by profession. I recall now, he studied at Cambridge and was at one point held as one of the greatest scientific minds of the generation regarding herbal remedies."

Holmes nodded, taking a large puff off his pipe.

"He was liberal in his practices, too," offered Holmes.

"Quite. It was his out-of-the-box thinking that caused him to fade from the medical light some time ago."

"Well, Watson. The answer to your original question, I will come as Dr Freud requested. Grotesque is not a word to be used lightly, and when a man of that calibre endorses it, it is worth investigating. I trust you will accompany me?" He puffed on his pipe, awaiting my answer.

"I most certainly will!"

*****

The next day, Holmes and I made our way to the Savoy Hotel on The Strand.

The man at the desk was expecting us, and we were shown to the Doctor's room immediately.

We were let in and told the Freud would be back shortly.

Holmes and I took a seat near a lit fire. Tea was made and brought to us. Both helped to fight against the chilly February day. Holmes paid little attention to refreshment while we waited for our caller. I had just finished my cup when a man emerged through an adjoining door.

"Mr Holmes," came a soft voice from the man. We both stood. A tall, finely dressed man with a thick peppered beard approached us. "Hallo. I am Dr Freud. I cannot tell you how grateful I am for your assistance," said the soft-spoken German doctor.

"It is our pleasure to meet you," said Holmes. "And this is my friend and colleague, Doctor John Watson."

"A pleasure," said Dr Freud. "Though I fear this case is very sensitive and I am reluctant to disclose information to anyone other than yourself, Mr Holmes."

"Fear not. What you say to me, you may say to Doctor Watson. Where I go, he goes," said Holmes in my defence.

Dr Freud paused for thought. "Very well. I trust your word, Mr Holmes," said he. "And Doctor Watson," he continued gently, "I meant no disrespect to your person."

"None was taken," I said. "This would not be the first time such a concern has been brought up." Doctor Freud smiled politely and motioned for us to take our seats.

With fresh cups of tea, we sat and listened to Dr Freud.

"I thank you for coming on such short notice. Forgive my mystery in the letter. I have learnt that it is best to keep some things simple when sending correspondence. You never know who may be peeking."

Holmes nodded and motioned for the doctor to continue.

"Now, the patient, Mrs Dabish," Dr Freud went on. "Let me tell you more about her. She comes from the United States. Virginia. It was there, some seven years ago, that she met her husband, Dr Dabish. The two were wed within weeks of meeting and moved to England. I suspect something of an Oedipus complex was at work with this whirlwind marriage. She was working as a governess for a rich family, and he had recently lost his mother…over which the two bonded."

"Bring us up to now, then," said Holmes.

"As I mentioned before, her husband disappeared nearly six months ago, and, in fact, the police have told her that he is dead."

"On what do they base this conclusion?" Holmes asked.

"Last anyone knew, he was going to spend some time hiking in the Lake District. They believe he fell and has been lost."

"It's been known to happen," I said.

"Yes, but there is something strange going on. I have learned of a small number of disappearances in the Dulwich area over the past few months. People who, it would seem, have no reason to up and leave nor abandon their families or homes; they just vanish."

"And you think Dabish is another one," Holmes said.

"Yes, well. I learnt that the Dabish's were well-loved and highly respected by the members of their community. Mrs Dabish's hysteria has come as a shock. Let me be clear, the authorities were very firm in their conclusion that there was absolutely no evidence pointing to anything other than a self-inflicted wound. The only testimony we have is from the maid, Veronica Smith, who said privately that Mrs Dabish took the disappearance of her husband hard."

"Naturally. Poor woman," said I.

"Who was the Inspector on the case?" Holmes asked.

"A man named Inspector William Daniels."

"Daniels is a respectable man," said Holmes. "That aside, it would seem you are under the impression something was missed?"

"Correct," Dr Freud continued. "Female hysteria is brutal for women, but this does not feel like so classic a case. Let me recall all the events so far. I was simply visiting London for recreation when this case was brought to me. Inspector Daniels heard I was in the city and sent someone to fetch me. I found this bothersome, as I was looking for a bit of peace after a tiresome year.

"I was told that Mrs Dabish was found by the housemaid, Miss Smith, and that she was lying on the kitchen floor with a knife in her chest. But still very much alive. Miss Smith tried to help Mrs Dabish, but she was unbearable and impossible to aid. As fate would have it, there lives a physician within earshot of the Dabish house. He was home and heard the cries. He came over to help and saw Mrs Dabish in this shattered state of mind. In addition to the self-inflicted wound, he told the police that she was rambling on about a devil and accused anyone who approached her of being a devil. He was able to sedate her and tend to her wound. The woman missed all her vital organs in her attempted suicide, but when she awoke in the hospital, she was as frantic as ever, rambling on about empty eyes, a devil, and repeating a series of numbers five-one-eight-one-eight-nine-nine."

"What does that mean?" I asked. "A safe combination?"

"Your guess is as good as mine as to what these numbers mean," said Freud.

"Your story is compelling, Doctor." Said Holmes. "Where did you first see Mrs Dabish?"

"I was under the impression that she was under careful watch in a hospital, but I soon discovered she was incarcerated in Bedlam. A barbaric place, hardly suitable for even the most degenerate of people. I shouldn't wonder if those in charge of that establishment are in more need of psychiatric care than the prisoners inside."

"I am inclined to agree with you, Doctor," said I.

"I expressed my concern to Inspector Daniels about treating a patient in this environment, but I did not have the power to remove her," Freud said. "Though I was able to acquire a small, private room and keep her in there, closed off from the lunacy of the establishment. My conditions were that they move her and give me a place to work, or I would leave. Inspector Daniels asked me to try to discover the reason for this woman's sudden mental break. He informed me that the day before, she was over at a couple's house for afternoon tea, and there was nothing out of the ordinary in her behaviour."

"And what did you discover?" I asked.

Dr Freud turned his gaze from Holmes and towards me. "She was put in a strait-jacket and sat in the room with me. Her eyes were wide and panicked, and her lips were peeling and bloody from incessant biting. She only spoke a little, but I recorded it. Let me play it for you."

"Play it?" I questioned.

"Yes, Dr Watson, a revolutionary technique. I wanted to try a new way to obtain and store all the audible evidence I needed from time spent with my patient by recording conversations. Though painful work, and not always completely successful, it has been most useful on the rare occasion that I have been able to employ this method," Doctor Freud informed.

"Truly remarkable!" said I as Freud rose and turned on a phonograph sitting on a table. It began to crackle and play. We heard the following:

Doctor Freud: Mrs Dabish? Mrs Dabish, can you look at me?

Mrs Dabish: I see... you... I see you.

Doctor Freud: Do you know where you are?

Mrs Dabish: Away from it. The devil can't find me here.

Doctor Freud: What devil is this?

Mrs Dabish: Devilish eyes - empty... cold...black! No... No, no, the devil can't get me here. I can't smell it here.

Doctor Freud: Mrs Dabish, do you recognise this?

Mrs Dabish: No! Get away! Don't come near me! Stay away!

There were loud crashes and other voices shouting as they tried to restrain Mrs Dabish before the recording ended.

Dr Freud turned the phonograph off and took his seat again.

"This was yesterday. She's barely improved. All I was doing was handing her a photograph of her and her husband, and she exploded the moment I reached out towards her."

"And you believe this reaction is a direct result of her current condition. Do you think she was attacked by some devil?" Holmes asked.

"Let us leave spiritual matters out of this, but I do believe she was attacked. Mr Holmes, I can tell you this: her mind is gone. The person she was cannot return, but pieces of that person still remain, and it is those pieces of her that are reacting spontaneously with painful and startling triggers. Whatever caused this hysteria, it has manifested as the 'devil.'"

"Before we carry on, I should like to speak with Mrs Dabish," Holmes announced.

11

"Very well, I assumed you would and arranged for us to see her shortly. I have a hansom waiting outside for us."

*****

The journey to Southwark was quick. We arrived at Bedlam and walked the corridors, following Dr Freud. The hospital had a disturbing air. Even Holmes, who was master of controlling his emotions, had an expression of displeasure.

We were taken to the room where Mrs Dabish was being kept.

"Let me go alone. Listen through the slots if you must, but it would be best for me not to have any distractions," said Holmes.

"As you wish," said Dr Freud.

Holmes went inside, and Freud and I listened.

"Mrs Dabish?" Holmes said.

"The devil lurks." She said in a low, hissy tone. "Stalking his prey. Feeding on the innocent. I pray to God, save me. I pray. No one is safe, safe, no one is safe. No, I am safe now. God saved me."

"Mrs Dabish, may I speak with you?" Holmes asked.

"Yes ... yes, that's me, I'm Mrs Dabish," she replied in a gentle, American accent. "Please come in for some tea, won't you?" Looking through the slots, one could see that Mrs Dabish believed herself to be somewhere else.

Holmes walked over slowly and knelt down.

"I am Mr Sherlock Holmes; I need to ask you some questions."

"Homes, home, home no, no home, I can't go home! I am home! New home; no devil here. The devil hides in the shadows! I smell his breath!" The woman who was beginning to panic.

"Mrs Dabish, stay calm," Holmes interrupted.

"Isabelle, no one calls me Isabelle! My grandmother, she was Isabelle, too."

"Isabelle," said Holmes in a gentle voice. "Tell me about the devil." There was silence for some time, then Mrs Dabish's voice was heard.

"The devil smells. I can smell it. Could smell it."

"But you cannot smell him any more?" Holmes asked.

"No, smell. Yes, I had to get away from the devil's breath."

"Where did you smell him?"

"Everywhere," she said.

"What can you tell me of the devilish eyes?"

"The eyes," she said, her voice starting to shake. "The devilish eyes. I saw them, so empty, so black! It got me. It... it... got me! Got me, caught me. I run and run and run, but can't escape it. It chases, with cold, empty eyes! He says, five-one-eight-one-eight-nine-nine. Five-one-eight-one-eight-nine-nine. No, stop it! I'm safe, I won't go back! No! Leave me alone!"

Mrs Dabish started to flail, and Holmes quickly reached the other end of the room, where we opened the door and got him out. The moment the door shut, her face pressed against the slots, and she continued, "The devil will kill! He'll kill with sharp teeth and giant claws!"

She withdrew and continued mumbling the series of numbers Five-one-eight-one-eight-nine-nine until she calmed down.

We vacated the area, but we could still hear Mrs Dabish raise her voice from time to time as we departed. "What can you make of it, Mr Holmes?" asked Dr Freud, who got no reply.

Outside in the cold, late afternoon air, Dr Freud pressed again, "Mr Holmes, what do you think?"

"I am in agreement with you," he said. "She is a victim of a crime, one of which I will get to the bottom. Watson and I are off at once to the Dabish house in Dulwich."

"I should come with you!" said Dr Feud.

"Please, for now, do not," Holmes said. "Any urgent messages, send them to Baker Street. I will retrieve them there."

"What do you suspect, Mr Holmes?" asked Dr Freud urgently.

"I must gather as much data as I can; there is hardly enough to build any solid facts upon, bricks and clay and all that!" Holmes leapt into the hansom that was waiting for us.

"We will be in touch soon," said I, shaking Dr Freud's hand and following quickly behind Holmes.

Dulwich

Holmes did not utter a word the entire journey. He sat in solemn thought, smoking a cigarette while looking out the window. By the time we reached the Dabish house, the hour was coming upon eight o'clock, and the sun was long gone. The house was large and backed onto the woods, enclosed by a brick wall. There was a small barn in the back garden. As we came up the drive, we could see a figure, which I assumed to be the housemaid, walking back to the house from the barn holding a lantern. When the figure saw us, it raced inside the house.

Holmes and I approached the front door and knocked. The maid greeted us. Her face was flushed.

"Good evening, Miss Smith. I am Sherlock Holmes, and this is my colleague, Doctor Watson. We are investigating the events that occurred the other day with Mrs Dabish. I hoped to speak with you about the incident."

"I've said all I can about it," said Miss Smith.

"If you will indulge me, Miss. May we come in?"

"The house is in a bit of disarray. Might you come back tomorrow when Ah've had a chance to clean up a bit more?"

"I must strongly protest to any further cleaning before I have had a chance to look around," Holmes said sternly.

She opened the door and reluctantly let Holmes and I enter.

"Please take us to where you found Mrs Dabish the other day," he ordered, and we followed her through the parlour into the kitchen.

"Was in here," she said.

The kitchen was large and spacious. There was a stone cooker with some copper pots hanging by it. Next to the stone cooker was a small cutting table, a cabinet filled with dry goods, spices, and seasonings. The door that went down into the cellar was ajar slightly.

The maid confirmed that it was from here that Mrs Dabish pulled a knife to lay her blow upon herself.

"Tell me, where were you when Mrs Dabish injured herself?" Holmes asked.

"Ah was ironing clothes.."

"Was anyone else around?"

"No, it was just us two. It's only been the two of us for some time."

"Just you two, ever since Dr Dabish went missing, correct?" I asked

"That is so," she replied.

"What prompted you to come to the kitchen?" Holmes asked.

"Ah heard a yelp and wanted to see if ev'rything was all right," said the housemaid. "Ah came in and the Mrs was lying on the floor in great pain and a knife was sticking out of her chest. She was screaming and yelling and frantic about some devil, some numbers, but Ah've no idea what any of it meant. Ah screamed for help, and luckily, the doctor next door heard me and came over. He struggled with her for some time before managing to put her to sleep using some of the chemicals in Dr Dabish's study. Then she was taken to a hospital and that is the last Ah've heard."

"Thank you," said Holmes. "Would you mind pointing me in the direction of the Dabish's master bedroom and Dr Dabish's old study?"

"Yes, the study is down in the cellar here and the room is up stairs—the first door on the right."

"Thank you. If we need any more information, we will find you," said Holmes.

Miss Smith bowed and left through the parlour.

"Friend Watson," said Holmes the moment the maid left, "will you venture up into the master room and look for anything that might be of use? I will start here in the kitchen, then go into the cellar."

"Very well, Holmes." As I turned to leave, Holmes who spoke suddenly.

"What... is... this...?" As I turned back around he was lying on the floor looking under the island in the centre.

"What have you found?"

"A piece of paper," he said, standing up. I approached, and we both examined it. The little piece of paper had been ripped from what appeared to be a notebook and had on it, handwritten, the name: The Devil's Breath

"What is this devil's breath, I wonder?" said I, holding the paper in my hand.

"It is curious," Holmes said thoughtfully. "Carry on, Watson. Tell me what you find upstairs."

Upstairs, I made my way into the master room. When I opened the door, I found the maid inside rummaging around a small cabinet.

"Madam. I believe Mr Holmes asked you not to move or touch anything," I sternly informed.

"Apologies, sir, I was only tidying after my work from earlier," she replied and scampered out of the room.

I walked over to the small cabinet where she was rifling and opened the top drawer. There was nothing inside whatsoever.

I looked through the closets and other dressers, but had no luck at all with finding anything useful.

I was ever curious about what the maid was doing when I came in and decided to try to spy on her. I left the room and walked up the hallway, peeking in the other rooms. I noticed the maid was in another room toying about, but doing nothing of any real interest. I decided it was best to inform Holmes of my lack of findings.

When I walked past the master room, I was startled to see someone. I looked back, and it was Holmes.

"What are you doing?" I asked.

"Seeing if you found anything," he said.

"Unfortunately not," I replied. "What did you find?"

"There was nothing of great interest but some old scientific equipment down in the cellar belonging to Dr Dabish."

"Holmes," I said quietly, "the maid was in here fiddling with the small cabinet by the bed."

"Was she now?"

"I told her to stop, and she left the room. But I found nothing inside."

Holmes bent down and examined the cabinet. He opened the drawer and the door and found nothing inside. He knocked on the top and felt his hand around the inside of the drawer. Then he pulled the cabinet away from the wall and let out a slight groan, as if it were hooked on something. There was a crack, and half of its back broke off.

"It would seem you did miss something," said Holmes.

He motioned for me to look and there I saw several little holes in the back. But that was not all. There was a metal pipe which came up from the floor and went up into the drawer. Holmes felt around when something else clicked. A small compartment opened but nothing was inside.

"It would appear that the maid was covering something up."

Just then, we heard a loud roaring sound, and we raced to the room directly across the hall. Outside, in the back garden, the maid had started a large fire.

"We must stop her!" Holmes cried.

As fast as we could, we made our way outside, but did not see her. The only light was from the glow of the fire. There was another loud bang, and we saw the maid burst out of a barn and race past us on the back of a horse. I pulled out my revolver and took one shot. The horse let out a neigh but continued to run.

"She's gone," said Holmes. "I think it would be best for us to regroup and begin anew tomorrow. There was a public house on the main road. We should find a room there I trust."

Holmes, standing by the fire, began to sway and held his head in his hands a moment.

"Are you all right, Holmes?" I asked.

"I believe so, yes. Just dizzy. Come, let us be off," said he.

*****

The next morning, I was awakened by a knock on the door.

"Holmes, is that you?" I called, somewhat agitated by so early a disturbance.

"It is, Watson. Make yourself ready—we are summoned," he replied.

I rose from the hotel bed, my back a trifle stiff, and made what haste I could in preparing myself. I found

Holmes downstairs in the dining room, where he stood in conversation with two men. One was a police officer, and the other was Inspector Daniels.

"Ah, good morning, Watson. There have been new developments in the night," said Holmes, his grey eyes shining with interest. "Pray, Inspector, recount the events for us."

"Good morning, Doctor Watson," said the Inspector, as I inclined my head in greeting. "Last night, upon hearing that you had visited the Dabish house, I thought it prudent to remain nearby. The doctor who resides next door reports that he witnessed the events from his second-floor window. He claims to have seen the maid set a fire and observed you both attempting to restrain her, even to the point of discharging your revolver.

"Later in the night, there was a disturbance a short distance up the road, at the Whitehorn Estate. A woman, believed to be mentally deranged, was seen running about the grounds. I responded to the call, and what we discovered was that the Dabishs' maid had entirely lost her reason. We have no indication of the horse's whereabouts, nor of where she intended to go after charging at you."

"Utterly fascinating, is it not, Watson?" exclaimed Holmes, with evident delight.

"Not precisely the term I should employ," I remarked dryly.

"Where is the maid now?" Holmes inquired.

"She is in our custody at the local station, though she will be transferred shortly. Her condition is... unstable," the Inspector replied.

"Was there anything found upon her person?" Holmes pressed.

"A small journal," said the Inspector.

"I must see it. Can you procure it for me?" Holmes insisted.

"I can bring it to you, certainly. But, Mr Holmes, I must confess my displeasure that you chose to pursue a lead from Doctor Freud without notifying the proper authorities. If there is something amiss in the Dabish case—and I am now persuaded that there is—we must act in concert."

"We can come to such an arrangement," Holmes agreed smoothly. "Are we far from the Whitehorn Estate?"

"Only a few minutes' drive."

"Excellent. Then perhaps we might begin with an inspection of the Whitehorn Estate, if you would be so kind as to convey us there, Inspector."

"Very well. Come with me."

We entered the cart, and within ten minutes had arrived at the estate.

Inspector Daniels indicated to Holmes the spot where the maid had been apprehended, and likewise showed us where the householders had first observed her from their windows. Holmes dropped suddenly to the ground, like bloodhound. The grass was tall, and it was evident that some manner of struggle had taken place. He followed a set of tracks to and fro until he reached the rear of the house. They ran through the garden, where the maid's footprints were plainly visible.

"She came to the back door, you see?" said Holmes, indicating the marks. "But she came from the woods."

At the edge of the garden lay a dense stretch of woodland. Holmes traced the tracks as far as the boundary. Without a word, he plunged into the thicket and began to move with increasing speed. He was upon a scent now and would not be denied.

Then, without warning, he halted.

"Do you smell that?" Holmes asked.

"I am suffering from a cold, I fear," said the Inspector apologetically.

"I follow you, Holmes. There is something stale in the air," said I.

Holmes pressed on deeper into the wood, advancing so swiftly that we lost sight of him within moments.

"Holmes!" I called. "Holmes, where are you?"

"Here, Watson!" came his faint reply.

We soon found him standing over what appeared to be a great mound of earth. It was only upon closer inspection that I perceived its true nature.

"It seems we have found the horse," said Holmes, holding his sleeve across his face to ward off the stench.

"My goodness! This is horrendous!" exclaimed Inspector Daniels.

"Some might say grotesque. But here—observe this," said Holmes, gesturing towards the carcass.

The unfortunate animal bore a vast gash along its side, scored with enormous claw marks.

"What are we dealing with here?" I asked.

"It would appear that there is some devil lurking in these woods."

"Mr Holmes, this is most troubling. Some time ago we received reports of a large, almost white, feline creature roaming the area. We had no proof—only the accounts of frightened villagers."

"It would have to be a creature of considerable size. I should say a lion or a tiger," said I.

"But neither lion nor tiger is white—what, then, were they seeing?" asked Inspector Daniels.

"It cannot be dismissed, Inspector. There is either a large predator at large, or someone has taken great pains to simulate one. Its only connection to my case lies in its attack upon the maid's horse. She escaped—but not, it would seem, without first losing her reason, which is a most curious detail," said Holmes thoughtfully.

"Inspector—Mr Holmes—come and look at this!" cried an officer.

We hastened to where he stood. Between his feet lay a distinct impression in the soil—the unmistakable print of a large animal.

"Is it a lion?" he asked.

"This is conclusive. You most certainly have a large feline at large. Unfortunately, I have not the leisure to devote myself to this matter. I must obtain that journal from you, return to the Dabish house, and examine the remains of the fire in daylight," said Holmes.

"This will reflect poorly upon me, having dismissed those earlier reports," said the Inspector gravely. "Still, it is my responsibility, and I shall see it through. But, Mr Holmes, you must bear in mind—this creature is dangerous. It may well account for the recent disappearances."

"Oh, the thought has already occurred to me," said Holmes. "It would be prudent to determine whether any game hunters reside in the vicinity—and whether one of them has brought something back, lawfully or otherwise."

"A sensible course, Mr Holmes. I shall pursue this line while you continue with the Dabish case. I will have the journal sent to you—expect it later today at the Dabish house. And may it be understood, Mr Holmes, that for the remainder of this case, I formally retain your services in uncovering the truth?"

"We are in agreement, Inspector," said Holmes, as he turned away, leaving the Inspector and the officer beside the dead horse.

When we arrived at the Dabish house, we were greeted by a most unexpected figure: Dr Freud. He stood upon the porch with his hands deep in his pockets and his sleeves rolled up, as though he had been patiently awaiting our arrival.

"Hallo. Good day, Mr Holmes, Doctor Watson," said he, greeting us with a firm handshake.

"Doctor, what brings you here?" Holmes inquired.

"I have conceived an idea and wished to attempt an experiment," he replied, with a curious gleam in his eye.

"Ah, Dr Freud, you have brought the patient home."

I was utterly astonished at Holmes's conclusion, having no notion how he had arrived at it.

"Holmes, how can you know this?" I asked.

"There are scratch marks upon the good Doctor's hand. The wounds are fresh—the blood has not yet dried—indicating a recent struggle. The Doctor has brought Mrs Dabish here, hoping to use her shattered mind to reconstruct the events which deprived her of reason."

"Quite right youare, Mr Holmes," said Doctor Freud. "My assistants are upstairs watching over her now. She is confined to her room, which has been cleared of all harmful objects. And you are correct regarding the scratches—she resisted violently when we brought her inside." He winced slightly as he cradled his arm. "There is great risk in this course, but I hope that by returning her to this environment, we may extract some meaningful insight. It is not without danger, for she has taken to carving strange images upon the walls with her fingernails."

"What manner of images?" Holmes asked.

"A feline," the Dr replied.

"Curious," said Holmes. "If you will excuse me, I was unable last evening to conduct a thorough investigation of the house. I should like to resume it now."

"By all means. May I accompany you?"

"You may."

Holmes at once set about examining the kitchen. He lingered before the china cabinet, then turned his attention to the stone cooker. Bending low, he inhaled deeply and began to sift through the ashes. Producing a small envelope, he gathered a quantity of ash and secured it within his pocket.

"My friends, would you oblige me by examining the fire pit and determining what was burnt there?" he asked.

"Very well," said I, and Dr Freud and I withdrew.

Armed with stout sticks, we began to sift through the charred remains.

"Tell me," said I, "do you consider it wise to bring the poor woman back to this place? Might it not worsen her condition?"

He paused, and a shadow of concern crossed his features.

"It would be untruthful to deny the risk, Dr Watson. Yet we all have our methods—some accepted, others condemned. Some might think this unhelpful... yet, I will risk it."

"And what do you hope to gain?" I pressed, turning over fragments of burnt cloth and broken clay vessels.

"Mrs Dabish's mind is not wholly lost—merely fragmented as I said when we first met. If we can confront her with the sensations of that day—a smell, an image, an atmosphere—we may yet draw forth the truth. I see no reason for such a complete collapse without cause. If we can

26

identify the origin of this 'devil' she speaks of, we may uncover everything."

"What have you found?" Holmes called from a distance.

"Nothing beyond common household items—pots, clothing," said Dr Freud.

"A remarkable quantity of cooking materials," Holmes observed, kneeling beside the pit. "And a considerable amount of seasoning has been cast into the fire." He leaned closer and inhaled. "Do either of you detect anything unusual?"

We did as he asked. At once, I felt a dizziness steal over me.

"Curious, is it not?" Holmes remarked.

"It is—but what is it?" I asked.

"I shall conduct an experiment to determine that," said Holmes, collecting further ash and fragments of pottery. "Ah—and I obtained this whilst inside."

He handed me a small leather journal.

"Is this what Inspector Daniels recovered from the maid?"

"Indeed. I believe we have gathered sufficient evidence. Let us retire indoors and examine it."

"Gathered? Holmes, what have we gathered?" asked Doctor Freud.

"My dear Doctor, the threads are already weaving themselves together. The clues lie plainly before you."

*****

Seated in the parlour at a table, Holmes turned the pages of the journal. Freud and I were oppose Holmes. From the upside-down book, I noticed the handwriting was delicate.

Upon the first page was the inscription of Mrs Dabish herself. The entries detailed her private reflections. It was a strange sensation to rummage through the thoughts of a once rational woman, knowing that her broken mind now lingered upstairs.

Holmes read in silence until, suddenly—

"Aha!" He began to flip back and forth between pages. "Yes, yes…"

"What is it?" I asked.

"Mr Holmes?" Pressed Freud.

"A fragment of insight," said he, handing me the journal from his side of the table. I placed it down so that Dr Freud might read as well.

May '98

Walter has returned from the mainland, having first visited somewhere in the Midlands. He refuses to tell me what business he pursued, claiming it to be of a sensitive nature. He has brought animals for experimentation. I am uneasy. He spends ever more time in the cellar, and a most devilish odour emanates from it. It makes me ill.

June '98

I have begged Walter to move his experiments. The smell is unbearable. He grows angry and behaves most unlike himself. He makes frequent trips into the city and sends the maid upon secret errands. I shall follow him next time. For now, I shall retire to Chester and stay with my sister for a few weeks.

July '98

The house was in disarray upon my return. Walter was strange— distant. I followed him into Whitechapel. He entered a foul public house and later emerged with a hideous man, bald, with a scar upon his left cheek. An envelope passed between them. When I confronted Walter, he warned me to remain silent—for the sake of my sanity. He claims to have moved his laboratory, though he will not say where. Even with the smell gone, I remain unwell. I hear noises in the night. I shall return to Chester.

August '98
Walter appears more himself. He has redecorated the master room and introduced new foods. It is a welcome change, though my health remains poor. Yet he forbids all inquiry into his experiments.

September '98
Walter grows aloof once more. I saw him arguing upon the road with the same man from Whitechapel. I dare not ask questions. The meals make me ill—I have refused them. Last night I could have sworn I saw a beast, white as snow, beyond the window. This month is dreadful. I was awakened by a crash—the maid dismissed it. Yet I thought I detected that dreadful odour once more.

October '98
Walter has been gone for weeks. I dare not speak of our troubles. I fear for my mind—I hear growls and thunderous sounds at night. The smell has returned. The maid has been venturing into the woods for hours at a time. I intend to follow her. If only I could escape that smell —it is like—

….The page was torn, leaving the sentence unfinished.

Holmes leaned back. "A man of dual nature—this is not the first instance I have encountered such a case."

"I remember," I said, recalling to memory the events of our strange adventure with Dr Jekyll.

"So we now see the origin of her 'devil,'" said Dr Freud.

"She has named the smell as well," Holmes added.

"She has? I missed it," said I.

Holmes produced a small slip of paper he rescued from the kitchen upon our first visit and fitted it neatly into the torn page.

"The devil's breath, my dear fellows—that is the smell. Our difficulty, at present, lies in identifying its source."

"It lingered even after her husband vanished," I observed.

"A symptom, perhaps," said Dr Freud. "Trauma may produce such hallucinations."

"One possibility—but only a theory," Holmes replied. "Come."

He placed ash within the cooker and ignited it. Within minutes, a faint yet dreadful odour filled the air. My head swam violently.

"What is this infernal stench?" cried Dr Freud.

"Outside," said Holmes.

Once in the fresh air, he spoke:

"That was the scent of *radix pedis diaboli*—the Devil's Foot. You remember, Watson? How it came to be here remains to be determined. Yet this is not pure—it is combined with something else."

"How do we proceed?" I asked.

"The pipes, Watson—the pipes!"

Holmes set off upon a new line of inquiry, while Dr Freud resumed his experiment with Mrs Dabish. I accompanied him upstairs.

Mr Dabish sat on the floor, in a corner.

"Where is my cabinet?" she asked suddenly, staring at the empty walls across from her.

"It has been removed," he said.

"Was there something within it?" I asked, hoping to stir a memory.

Her eyes widened with terror.

"The devil… the devil…"

"How so?" Freud urged. He approached her slowly and squatted down.

"The devil, he lied…" she muttered.

But she soon fell silent. Freud and I shared a look.

"Would you care to walk about the house?" he asked.

She did not move for a few moments. Then she lifted herself up and walked over towards the door, past Dr Freud and me.

We began a tour through the house. We started with the rooms upstairs, but nothing seemed to interest her, so we took the woman down. As we descended, her agitation increased. In the parlour, her gaze fixed upon the kitchen.

"How do you feel?" I asked.

Suddenly she cried out: "The devil—he's here! I can smell him, I can smell him!"

Freud and I tried to hold her. He called for his assistants. She broke free and ran into the dining room.

Then came a scream—terrible beyond description.

"The beast!"

We rushed into the room. She was frozen, looking out the window. I turned to see and to my horror, there, in the yard, stood a monstrous feline—white as snow, marked with dark stripes. Surely this was the creature that had killed the maid's horse the night before.

I grabbed my revolver, watching the beast. Freud shouted for his assistants as he hurried the woman away to her room.

"Outside!" I said.

One of the assistants was crouching behind a large stone birdbath.

I rushed through to the back door. The creature eyed the young man, its large pink tongue licking its face. The young man saw me and shot towards the house. The beast crouched to spring. I fired my gun into the air, drawing its attention. The young man fell. The beast jumped back at the sound, but only for a moment before coming towards him, claws out. I fired again, striking it somewhere. With a snarl, it fled into the woods.

The young assistant rushed inside, and we shut the door.

Moments later, Holmes emerged from the cellar.

"I heard gunfire!"

"I saw it—the beast," said I. "Mrs Dabish first—and then I. It was a giant cat."

"Where was it?"

I pointed outside. Without a thought he went outside.

"Holmes!"

Holmes examined the ground.

"A blood trail. Crack shot, Watson. Let's tell Inspector Daniels at once, this beast needs to be found and dealt with so that no more harm comes to anyone or any thing."

"Holmes," called Dr Freud, from the backdoor, "there is something you should know—the cabinet—"

"The hidden compartment," I added.

"Precisely. I believe she concealed the journal there."

"And tore the page in fright, I shouldn't wonder," said Holmes. "And I," Holmes continued, "have discovered something further. Comes inside."

He moved the cabinet in the kitchen aside, revealing a concealed door. Slowly, he opened it to reveal a dark passage that stretched downward into the depths beneath the house.

Doctor Freud picked up a lamp. He quickly lit it, and the three of us descended below. The path was narrow and low. Each of us had to hunch over as we walked down the slope. It looked as if someone had started to build a separate cellar, but gave up almost immediately.

"Holmes, I wonder if Mrs Dabish knew about this area," I said. "I remember her casting very queer glances over at the china cabinet when Doctor Freud and I brought her down."

"That is a keen eye, Watson. This adds to the endless curiosities of this case. Here, mind your step, there is a drop," said Holmes.

A few moments later, we found ourselves in a very small opening. There were several copper pipes dangling from the ceiling, which connected to a large, round, metal oven-like object. There was an awful stench in the room. It was much stronger than the one we smelled upstairs during Holmes's experiment.

"Is this some kind of heating system?" Doctor Freud questioned.

"Negative. Mrs Dabish complained in her journal about smelling the devil's breath even after her husband vanished. This conduit system was feeding the smell into her room in what appears to be a gaseous form. Truly, very fascinating," affirmed Holmes, as he continued examining the metal sphere. "One thing is immediately clear; someone was using this fume to torment her."

"Holmes, there are footprints. Someone has been down here recently," said I. "Might it be the maid?"

"Is she responsible for all this? She is the one who tried to burn everything, took the journal, and ran away," Dr Freud said curiously.

"Yet, when she ran, she fell into the same fate as Mrs Dabish," said I.

"She was the keeper of some information; that much can be safely assumed. The prints on the ground are wider than hers, unless she wore a man's boots, size ten by the looks of them, while down here," said Holmes.

"I think we should bring Mrs Dabish down. I am interested in her reaction," Dr Freud admitted.

"Are you not worried what type of effect this could have on her already fractured mind?" asked Holmes.

"Mr Holmes, you know very well that not all methods are always carried out through conservative means," replied the Doctor. Holmes looked at Freud for some time before nodding slightly.

When we ascended from the cellar, we heard a knock at the front door. I answered, and a young police officer stood before me.

"Is Mr Holmes here?" he asked.

"Yes, this way," said I, showing the young man into the parlour.

"Mr Holmes, I have something for you from Inspector Daniels," said the officer, handing over a note. Holmes took it swiftly and read through it.

"It seems the maid, in her delirium, has mentioned something about a dark figure with empty eyes and ramblings of a broken heart." Holmes folded the note up and put it in his pocket. He stood for some time, lost in thought. I asked the officer if that was all the information he had for us.

"It is, and I must be on my way," said the officer, and I showed him the way out. When I returned, Dr Freud was making his way upstairs.

"Holmes asked me to get Mrs Dabish," said he. I nervously walked back into the parlour and waited.

Mrs Dabish was brought back downstairs. I could see a look of nervousness when she entered the parlour, as her eyes shifted towards the window, then quickly over to the china cabinet. Seeing the cabinet moved aside and the doorway opened, she convulsed back in an attempt to avoid going any further.

"No... can't go in there... No... won't do it!" she cried.

"What is your fear?" Doctor Freud asked. "Why don't you want to go inside?"

"No, no! I can smell it, the devil's here! He came from down there!" she cried.

"Who is the devil?" asked the Doctor.

"The devil lied; he lied to me. All this time, a great lie! No!"

"Who lied to you? What did the devil do?" Freud asked firmly.

The poor woman was resistant to going any further. She was violently shaking back and forth, trying to free herself.

"What did he look like?" demanded Holmes. I thought his interjection to be poorly timed and insensitive to the woman's condition. There have been times in my career with Holmes when I strongly disagreed with his approach to achieving results.

"Eyes, big eyes. Empty eyes! Oh, that awful smell! The lies! I'll tell the world! I told him I would! I told him!" she cried, and burst into a fury which caused one of the assistants to lose his grip on her. She bit the other and hurled herself through the parlour window. "I know where you are!" she screamed, her demented voice echoing in the evening air.

We chased after her as she bolted through the back garden and into the woods behind the house. I had never seen such madness in all my life. With the sun gone, it was very difficult to find the lost woman. My mind constantly returned to the thought of the giant feline that we had seen. With a cry that sounded like the bowels of hell opening up, I heard one final outburst from Mrs Dabish, and then all was silent.

"Holmes!" I cried.

"Here, Watson," he returned, a few yards ahead. I found him and Doctor Freud catching their breath. "We must find her. She is the hound; she's on the scent and will lead us where we need to go."

"Where do we need to go? Holmes, what are you withholding from us?" demanded Freud.

"The secret lies in these woods, I believe. That's why the maid went there. She knew!" said Holmes. Another cry erupted some way ahead of us from one of Freud's assistants. "Watson, please get your revolver out," said Holmes.

Just then, the assistant came running towards us; we could see he was foaming at the mouth and appeared to have lost his sanity.

"We must press on! Let us spread out and move forward!" Holmes said sternly, and went off in the direction that the assistant had just come from. We slowly crept through the eerie woods, taking great care with every step to move quietly.

"Holmes!" I whispered. He walked over to me. "Someone is there." Far ahead, a figure moved among the trees. It, too, appeared to be looking for movement in the woods.

"Let's circle him," Holmes said, patting me on the back and quietly walking away.

We all crept around the figure, but something caught its attention, and it took off running. We chased after it with all haste. In a small clearing was a cabin, which the figure entered. Holmes instructed Dr Freud and his other assistant to stay outside while he and I went in. The cabin itself looked rather small, but Holmes noticed an oddity in the wooden floor. Pulling at the panels, he discovered a hatch. We opened it and found a small hole with a ladder. We descended and discovered a well-equipped laboratory.

Holmes moved around the room, inspecting everything. He found a piece of paper covered in notes.

"It is a chemical compound, Watson, extracted from the devil's foot root and turned into a vicious toxin that causes immediate hysteria when exposed in a large dose," said Holmes. Suddenly, and with a great jerk, I was ambushed! Someone had wrapped an arm around my neck and restrained me.

"Touch anything, and you will die!" said a muffled voice. I could see from the corner of my eye that my assailant was wearing a rubber mask of some type, which blacked out his eyes. They looked devilish and empty.

"The game is up, I'm afraid," said Holmes coolly, as he continued to walk around the room, stopping in front of a large metal door.

"Move again, and I will kill your companion," said the man.

"Kill him in the same manner you did Mrs Dabish or the maid?" asked Holmes.

"You know nothing," said the man.

"On the contrary, I know everything. You may as well take the mask off, Dr Dabish! For, as we speak, the authorities are on their way," said Holmes.

The man pushed me violently, and I fell into the table ahead. When I turned around, I saw he was wearing a fireman's air respirator. The mask covered his face, and the eye-pieces were two large, round, menacing cylinders. He looked haunting in this suit. He slowly pulled the mask off, revealing his face. It was indeed Dr Dabish.

"How did you know?" he asked.

"A journal left by your wife and found by your maid, who has incidentally lost her mind as well. Your wife's journal told the whole story. She revealed your odd behaviour after your trip to the mainland and your experiments in the cellar. She also told of the figure you were spotted with in Whitechapel and again in Dulwich. She spoke of the smell that made her ill and her demand that you move your experiments elsewhere. It was not just the smell, though, but the food. You began dosing her meals with various compounds to test your drug, disguising it in new foods as you pretended to reform.

"Upon my investigation of the house, I found evidence for the use of devil's foot root and a pipe which curiously funnelled the fumes up into the master bedroom. It was clear that someone was using these toxic fumes on Mrs Dabish. When she could still smell the aroma after your apparent disappearance and supposed death, it was clear that you were not gone. You created a devilish chemical. You needed someone to test it on; who better than your wife, the woman standing in the way of you and the maid, Miss Smith?

"Oh yes, it is mentioned in the journal how she took the blame for loud noises at night, noises that were really from you and your terrible experiment. She also mentioned how you sent the maid on secret trips; how she, too, would often sneak away into the woods with no explanation as to where she would go after you were gone. But your wife had too much pride, and you were too well respected in the community to reveal any trouble within. She was in your pocket the entire time, but something went wrong. She discovered you were alive. She found you coming out of the secret cellar where you were storing the fumes. When you saw her, you dosed her with a near-lethal amount that shattered her mind. In return, she tried to kill herself to escape the torment and pain," said Holmes. The man looked at us with great fear and anger in his eyes. "Is it not true?"

"For the most part, what you say is true," said Dr Dabish. "Although I did not attack her without reason, she discovered Miss Smith and me by mistake. On a day when my wife was meant to be gone, she followed Miss Smith into the woods after I sent her to fetch something for me. Miss Smith noticed her and tried to get back in time to warn me. When my wife caught us in the kitchen, she burned with such anger. She attacked Miss Smith, so I…" Dr Dabish held up a small capsule, "…exploded this in her face. The effect was strong, and she was immediately sent into hysterics. It was then, in her psychotic state, that she took a knife and shoved it into her chest." Dabish smiled when he stopped. "She was making so much noise. When I heard the doctor from next door come over, I hid, and Miss Smith took care of the rest. Her hands were muddy, so the alibi of being in the garden worked. But my work, oh, good sir, is far bigger than you could ever imagine. With my work, the world will burn and be reborn."

"I care not for your deluded ideas. Tell me, where is Mrs Dabish? It was you who took her into the woods. Where did you put her?" Holmes demanded.

"She's through that door," said Dr Dabish, looking defeated.

Holmes opened the heavy metal door, and what we found on the other side horrified not only me, but Holmes also. Lying in a pool of blood was Mrs Dabish, and in the corner was the giant feline. Upon closer examination, the beast looked like a tiger, only white as snow. Its fur was covered in the crimson of blood. In the corner were several other bodies, potentially those Freud and Inspector Daniels had mentioned as missing. Holmes turned back, his eyes burning with anger towards Dr Dabish.

"You see, sir, it doesn't matter who is coming, because they will only find you dead and me gone. Even if they know I'm alive, I am protected by very powerful people," said Dabish, who was walking around the table that separated us from Holmes. He reached in his pocket, pulled out a gun, and pointed it towards Holmes. "Get inside the room. You too!" he said, turning towards me. In the moment that Dabish turned his head, Holmes lunged at the man.

The revolver, which was now aimed at the ceiling, went off and stirred the feline. In a flash, Holmes pushed him against the wall. Dabish then pulled a lever. I could hear the sound of an engine coming to life. I reached for my revolver. The mad doctor managed to push Holmes through the door. He was shutting it when I fired a shot at his arm. He fell forward, and Holmes grabbed him. The big cat roared and began to move. Holmes grabbed Dabish, spun, and released him. He fell backwards into the room where his dead wife lay, and the cat lurked. Hearing a powerful release of air from a conduit system, Holmes shut the door with Dabish and the feline inside. After a few moments, Dabish began pounding on the door hysterically while screaming. Then, with a horrific gulp, he went silent. All we could hear was the sound of the animal feeding.

We crawled out to find Doctor Freud and his assistant still waiting. We told them what had transpired as we made our way to the local police station, where we found Inspector Daniels sitting at a desk, going through reports.

"Hello, Mr Holmes, how are you?" asked Daniels. He looked up and saw our ruffled state. "Good Lord, what has happened to you?" he exclaimed.

"We seem to have found your rogue feline," said Holmes. We proceeded to tell Daniels about our venture and warned him of the cat trapped inside the cell, along with the bodies of Dr and Mrs Dabish and his traitorous chemical work. Inspector Daniels planned to extract the bodies the following day. We learned later that before the authorities could salvage the bodies, there was a tremendous explosion that demolished the entire structure, destroying all of Dabish's work.

*****

Upon our return to Baker Street, we were accompanied by Doctor Freud. While we sat in the study, Mrs Hudson served us a warm cup of tea.

"I believe your opening words, 'a grotesque affair', were almost prophetic," said Holmes to Freud.

"I would not suggest any type of supernatural ability, Mr Holmes. My powers, like yours, come from endless mental training and experimentation. I am eager for the day humanity can reject God and put faith in reason," he returned.

"Yes, but can reason answer all questions? There is nothing greater than the use of deductive reasoning in religious matters, my good Doctor Freud," said Holmes.

"Come now, Mr Holmes, we live in a world of science. Spiritual matters are for the infant mind. People who wish not to think for themselves."

"Science is not merely a tool for disproving religion. I believe there is too much goodness in the world. There is too much detail and beauty for science to be the only answer," said Holmes. "Rather, science is pointing to something greater."

"Time will tell. If anything, this case has shown the truly evil side of humanity," said Dr Freud.

"There is something about the case which we never found out, though. Mrs Dabish uttered a set of numbers. What did they mean?" I asked.

"I have wondered that myself. Mr Holmes, have you any more tricks up your sleeve?"

"I wish I did, but, unfortunately, the numbers are a complete mystery which I cannot solve," said Holmes thoughtfully.

"That is a shame. Still, tragic though the affair was, we got all the answers we needed," admitted Doctor Freud.

"I fear none will believe that animal we saw. It looked like a white tiger, but that is impossible," said I.

"One can only guess, but I have heard rumours of white tigers in my travels, Watson, though I have never seen any in person. There are many mysteries that still surround Dr Dabish," said Holmes.

"I could not agree more," said I.

"This case, Watson, will fall between those solved and those which remain open. I would like to know how Dabish got hold of the devil's foot root, what his overall scheme was, and what those numbers poor Mrs Dabish mentioned mean."

"Well, Mr Holmes, I thank you for your time and effort in this matter. I have already overstayed my visit to London and must return home," said Freud, standing up and putting on his coat. "I trust we will remain in contact." Holmes smiled, nodded, shook Doctor Freud's hand, and saw him out. Walking back into the study, Holmes held a piece of paper in his hand.

"What do you have there?" I asked.

"It's a souvenir from our recent endeavour. The moment before we left, I took this piece of paper with some of Dabish's notes," said Holmes, handing it over to me. "I will file it away and hope its mysteries may yet be discovered." Looking at the paper, I observed that it was part of a scientific formula that Dabish had been working on.

"I don't recognise this, Holmes. What is Petrus?" Holmes took the paper back into his hands.

"It's a curiosity. Latin, but I'm not aware of its meaning, and sadly, Watson, the 'what' may never be answered, not without more data."

A STUDY IN YELLOW

The Problem of Mr & Mrs Applegate

It was March of 1899. All of London rejoiced in the splendid sunny weather. Though many were happy to enjoy the improved climate, there was a feeling of unease. The newspapers were full of the ongoing story. Three young women, all in their early twenties, had been missing since January. One, named Edith Smith, was the daughter of George Smith, a wealthy businessman who owned several manufactories across the country. The second woman was Marge Owens. Her family was of Welsh origin and had moved to London in 1880, when her father, Francis Owens, began a prestigious job with the British government. The third was Sandra Vanders, whose father owned a shoemaking shop called 'Vanders', located near Leicester Square. This shop was regarded as one of the best in the city and received business from many of London's finest.

Since the start of the New Year, the police had turned over every stone, gone down every dark alley, and searched every river bank within the greater London area to no avail. There were simply no clues to follow. It appeared that these young women had simply vanished into thin air. On a daily basis, the parents of the missing women posted advertisements in all the papers, pleading for information from anyone who might shed some light on bringing their daughters home, along with a hefty reward offered in return. I recall Holmes was questioned in the matter towards the end of January, just after the third woman had gone missing. Even with his great powers of deduction, there was no solid evidence to point him in a specific direction. Not even a simple connection between the three could be made. The families knew nothing of each other until these terrible events brought them together. Holmes concluded that the only connection must lie within the kidnapper himself. He, and he alone, must hold the key. Therefore, with no other leads to follow, Holmes left the matter in the capable hands of Lestrade.

*****

In the study of 221b Baker Street, Holmes and I indulged in our standard routines. I was in my chair, reading the newspaper, which was filled with the events of the missing women and Scotland Yard's earnest promise that they were hard at work on the case. Holmes, however, was seeing to his chemicals, which he had been poring over since the previous night.

"If this works, Watson, I will have saved a man's life from the hangman's rope," he said, mixing solutions. "The case hangs on the type of two blood stains found on the man's shoe. You know the case, Watson, the man accused of killing his servant."

"Is this good news?" I asked.

"We shall know shortly, though it seems… wait a moment, Watson," he paused to look over his findings. "Ah, well, yes, there we have it, just as I thought. You see, the servant was found, a bloody mess, deep in the city. The man claimed to be out all day and nowhere near that part of the city, but in his house were a pair of shoes with blood on them. Therefore, the only proof used to convict the man was the blood stains on his shoe. When I spoke to the man, he mentioned that he had visited a butcher's shop on the day of the murder. The blood on the shoe, though suggestive, is not human blood. This clears the man's alibi, and I'm almost certain it was his brother who killed the servant. I must speak with Detective Williams straight away on the matter." Holmes shot up from his chair and desk, leaving his Bunsen burner lit, grabbed his coat, and was out the door. When the room had calmed, I resumed reading.

*****

Holmes had been gone several hours when a tiny knock on the study door pulled me away from my paper.

"Yes, come in," I called. Mrs Hudson poked her head in the door.

"Doctor, there are guests here for Mr Holmes."

"I am afraid he is out, and I'm unsure when he will be returning."

"They are very persistent. Might they speak with you in his absence?" Reluctantly, I agreed and put the paper down. Mrs Hudson showed the guests into the study, and I motioned for them to take a seat. "Thank you," said the couple in unison.

"I will bring you some drinks," Mrs Hudson offered, leaving the room with a smile.

"Thank you, Mrs Hudson." I greeted the seated couple with a smile. "I'm afraid Mr Holmes is not here at present. I would be happy to take a message."

"And you are?" asked the man.

"Forgive me. I am Doctor John Watson, associate of Mr Holmes."

"He is the one who writes the stories," the woman said to her partner.

"Right. Well, Doctor Watson, my wife is the one who insisted we come see you, or Mr Holmes rather," he informed me.

"I have read a fair number of your exploits with Mr Holmes, and of course, we have seen both your names grace the newspaper a number of times. We need Holmes's help," said the woman.

"As I said, you are welcome to leave a message with me, and I will pass it along to Holmes when he returns. I dare not offer any more than that. Holmes is a busy man, and I cannot comment on his availability."

"Very well, Doctor Watson," said he. "My name is Edward Applegate, and this is my wife, Martha."

"Applegate, I recall the name," I began.

"I should hope so. I am very well known throughout the city and beyond. I am a thriving entrepreneur, currently funding projects in both the automobile and electricity markets," he informed me with great pride in his voice. "You may have heard I had a custom automobile built for the Royal Family," he boasted further. His wife nudged him to keep to the point and continue. "All that is void now. I am sure you have seen the papers these past few months riddled with news of young women who have gone missing."

As Mr Applegate spoke, his wife's face flushed red, and her eyes began to well up with tears. Soon, streams of water sped down her cheeks.

"It will all be fine, my dear." Mr Applegate tried to assure her. To me, he said, "Well, Doctor, our very own daughter, Rena, has gone missing and has been gone for three weeks now. She was returning from a holiday in Bristol, where we have some family, and she was meant to arrive by the 2:20 train on Saturday, the last, at Paddington

Station. Our immediate thought was that she had decided to extend her stay and had sent a letter that we had missed. When we returned home, we found nothing. My wife sent our relations a quick note to enquire about our dear Rena, and we received a telegram not long after saying she was put on the train. That is all we know of our sweet little girl," ended Mr Applegate.

"Can you help us, Doctor? Do you think Mr Holmes can look into this? Price is not a problem!" Mrs Applegate cried.

"Money is of no matter to me. Besides, my wages are fixed," Holmes's voice came from the study door as it slowly opened. "Your story is interesting. I heard it all from behind the door and did not wish to interrupt once you began your tale. Do forgive my dramatics." He walked in carrying the tray of drinks that Mrs Hudson had promised. "There is a reign of terror over all of London with these kidnappings. I cannot say at this time that your daughter is a victim of the same kidnapper, but my schedule is clear, as I have no other pressing case at the moment; thus, I will look into this delicate matter."

"Oh, Mr Holmes, thank you, deeply!" Mrs Applegate exclaimed, still fighting back a flood of tears, unsuccessfully.

"Anything that you need, Mr Holmes, please tell us," she asked.

"Well, I will need access to your property and to your daughter's rooms. There could be some clue to her disappearance hidden there. First, though, tell me about your daughter. What she looks like, what her habits are, her social circles, and any person of interest in her life," said Holmes.

"Rena is slim, about five feet five inches," Mr Applegate began. "She has natural red cheeks and has no need for these cosmetics that girls put all over themselves. Her hair is blonde; it can look white in some lights. As for her habits, her weekends are mostly spent at social clubs in Kensington, a short walk from our house."

"She spends her Sundays with us," Mrs Applegate added. "We attend St Paul's, in Covent Garden, and afterwards retire to someone's house for a late lunch. Her weekdays are spent in and around our home, with no real pattern or schedule other than teaching piano on Wednesday afternoons. Beyond that, she will go to the markets, have afternoon tea with friends…" Mrs Applegate raised her hand to her chin, thinking. "That seems to be all."

"And is there anyone of interest in her life? Any male attention?" asked Holmes.

"Great Scot! I should say not!" roared Mr Applegate with great force. "She is a very respectable young woman."

"I am not accusing her, sir, but these are things I must know if I am to find your daughter." Mr Applegate, whose face was fiery red, began to flush out, and his breathing calmed.

"My apologies, Mr Holmes, for my outburst, but to answer your question, no, there is no one of interest," he calmly returned.

"Mrs Applegate, do you know of anyone?" Holmes pressed.

"Mr Holmes! Is my word not good enough that you have to disrespect me to my face? I have told you there is no one, therefore there is no one!"

"I mean no disrespect, but keep in mind, females will reveal more to their mothers than to their fathers. Now, Mrs Applegate, please answer the question."

"No, there is no male attention in her life, Mr Holmes," said she, shaking her head quickly and answering in a quiet, mouse-like voice.

"And tell me, why was it that she was on holiday and you two were not?"

"She wanted to get out of the city for a bit. We have family further south. She thought a break to go and see them would be nice," Mr Applegate informed us.

"Thank you," said Holmes. "I should need to see her rooms at once if I am to take this any further."

There was a knock at the door, and Inspector Lestrade walked in. "Holmes, I'm sorry to interrupt, but may I speak with you a moment?" he asked.

"Very well." The two men stepped out into the hallway, and Holmes shut the study door behind him, leaving us unable to overhear their conversation.

A few moments later, Holmes returned with a face like stone.

"Mr and Mrs Applegate, there is something that I must see to right away. I will call upon you at your residence in Kensington. Please write down the full address," he said, handing Mr Applegate a slip of paper and a pencil. "We shall see you tomorrow morning around nine o'clock."

"What is so pressing, Mr Holmes?" roared Mr Applegate. "Have we not hired you?" As he spoke, he angrily wrote down his address with such force that I thought the pencil might snap.

"When you hire me, you hire my ways. I often see to more than one case. It is my practice to see matters through in my own manner, with no questions about my methods. Now, a certain situation has arisen in which I must accompany Inspector Lestrade immediately. A situation that could shed light on your particular issue, so if you will kindly excuse us, we must be off. We will see you in the morning," finished Holmes. Mr and Mrs Applegate stood up and walked out. Lestrade was still in the hallway waiting.

"What's the situation?" I asked.

"Three women have been found dead. Possibly the same three who were kidnapped, which could mean it was all the work of the same kidnapper, a devious figure who lurks in the shadows. It would be wise to look into the matter," said Holmes, grabbing his coat and hat as he followed Lestrade out of the door, and I right behind them.

*****

It was in a small, damp alley off Aldgate High Street where three female bodies lay. They were covered in blood, their faces heavily mutilated, their heads shaved, and they had large lacerations on their stomachs and chests. Each body was of similar build and matched the reports of the missing women. There was a further oddity; each victim had her left hip branded with a stylised 'Z'.

"The women were found about an hour ago. The coroner is on his way, but as of yet no medical personnel have examined the bodies. We have not had any medical opinions made yet, thus, Dr Watson, mind offering any opinion as to the time of death?" asked Lestrade. I bent down and examined one of the bodies which lay atop the morbid pile. At once, I noticed the women were covered in severe bruising.

"It would appear that they suffered some great physical trauma. Some of these bruises are quite old. I can see they all seem to suffer from some type of blunt force trauma, meaning they were abused regularly, not simply before death. Judging by the cut wounds, though, I would put the time of death at about eight to ten hours ago," said I.

"This woman is certainly one of the missing ones," said Holmes.

"What makes you so sure?" asked Lestrade.

"This one here, she has a large birthmark on her inner arm. That was in the report you gave me some time ago when you first asked me to look into the matter." Holmes exposed the birthmark hidden by one of the deceased ladies.

"Yes, I do remember that now. Why kidnap these women, shave their heads, brand them, then kill them and dispose of the bodies as such?" asked Lestrade, more in retrospect than anything else.

"Who found the bodies?" I asked.

"The owner of the shop here. Said she saw the pile as she passed the alley, and when she investigated and found this, she contacted us immediately," said Lestrade.

"The alley can be seen from the main road; no one else has reported seeing anything at all," I pressed.

"The blood, Watson, the blood," Holmes interjected. "If you will observe the cuts these women suffered, it would have caused a large amount of blood to spill, leaving quite the mess upon the ground where we now stand. Notice there are only small pools of blood around the victims. The amount of blood is key. And here by this window," Holmes moved over to a small window in the adjacent building and pulled out his magnifying glass to examine a few small stains, "you can see where a few drops of blood have fallen. Thus, it would seem obvious that they were defenestrated after their deaths."

"Do you suspect the shop owner of lying?" asked Lestrade.

"We should look around inside," Holmes returned.

"Very well," said Lestrade.

Soon, we were inside the small back room of the shop from which Holmes believed the women were tossed. The building itself was nothing of great interest. It was merely a small shop called Bessie's Boutique. Holmes searched the room for any more clues but found nothing. The shop owner, a middle-aged woman named Mrs Bessie James, informed us that she was the only person who worked in the shop and could not say who else might have been inside other than a vandal, as she and her husband were out at the theatre the previous night.

"It would be helpful if we could speak with your husband regarding the evening's events," said Holmes.

"Oh, of course, I will do my very best to cooperate with the law," said Mrs James. "I will close up shop and take you to see my husband straight away." She was excused as she began to close her store.

"She doesn't seem like someone who is hiding anything, Mr Holmes. I'm not sure someone forced these bodies out the window," admitted Lestrade, as the shop owner saw to her duties.

"Inspector, I must leave this with you for now. I need to follow another avenue with another case. Inform me if any new revelations are revealed," said Holmes.

"Is that it?" asked Lestrade. "Don't you have anything else?"

"Not at this stage."

"Very well, I will walk you out," said Lestrade, and we moved towards the door. "I will keep you informed. I can't fathom who would do such a horrible thing."

"The criminal mind is indeed a twisted and demented thing. Trying to understand it would take an eternity," remarked Holmes.

"This is all very similar to the horrible events in Whitechapel. It will surely send the public into a frenzy once word gets out. I do not wish that horror to be repeated. This cannot continue!"

"We will do our best to make sure that does not happen, Lestrade," Holmes assured. "I believe, however, that we are only scratching the surface. This situation is far from over."

"What do you mean?" asked Lestrade.

"Do inform me of your findings with Mr James," said Holmes, ignoring Lestarde's questions. "We can compare notes when I have had a better chance to conduct my own research."

Lestrade swallowed hard and then agreed. We hailed a hansom and were ushered back to Baker Street.

*****

Once back in the study, Holmes pulled out several documents and newspapers and laid them on the table. He studied them intently, saying very little and groaning occasionally when he stumbled on items of interest. I picked up a book and began to read. While I was deeply engrossed in the story, I was startled by the loud thud of Holmes slamming his open palm upon the desk.

"Watson!" exclaimed Holmes. I turned and saw him leaning over the desk; his face was bright with the illumination of some fact.

"What is it?" I snapped, as my heart began to recover from the shock of Holmes's excitement. Just before he spoke, Mrs Hudson entered the study.

"Everything all right up here?" she asked.

"Yes, sorry if I startled you, Mrs Hudson."

"Only ever so slightly, Mr Holmes. My real purpose in coming up here was to bring you this; it just came in the late post," said she, handing him a letter.

"Thank you." Holmes took the letter and tore it open.

"Would you like anything to eat or drink?" she asked.

Holmes was non-responsive, but I turned to Mrs Hudson and asked for some tea. When she left the room, I looked to Holmes, who was still reading. He put the letter down and grimaced.

"Is everything in order, Holmes?" I asked. "You were going to enlighten me about something."

"Oh, yes, I apologise. I have just received a letter from a source whom I have not spoken to in some time. Years, in fact."

"Who might this be?"

"You will remember him well. It is the infamous Fred Porlock."

"Porlock?! The man responsible for attempting to tip us off all those years ago, in the case of Mr Douglas's murder?"

"Yes, Watson, the very same one you entitled *The Valley of Fear*. That was the last correspondence I had with him. I feared the worst had befallen him. Though now it seems he is up to his old tricks again, giving us another cypher. We have not had such a busy day for some time!" said he excitedly. "Oh, and the commonality between all the young women thus far, including Miss Rena Applegate, is that they each have blonde hair."

Holmes did not bother to make eye contact with me. He simply remained focused on the letter from Porlock. "Blonde hair, you say. Holmes, I can hardly see how that is of any use to us!"

"It is an observation, Watson."

"What is this note from Porlock then?"

"It's cryptic text."

"Cryptic, eh? Porlock is on good form then," said I, standing up and walking over to Holmes to look at this new letter. This was written:

DQEHSUHSHTQNODELEESHSKFNMRGEOWDF SEUDHHOEK

At the bottom, it was signed by Fred Porlock.

"What does it mean?" I asked. Holmes fingered the note for some time. He appeared somewhat confused by the letter. "This does not appear to be another book cypher, though."

"Now that we have a firm grasp of the obvious, perhaps we can focus our mental energies on figuring out what the hidden message is. One glaring problem is tying our hands, much like before. We are void of the one thing we need: the key. Without that, we are helpless."

Holmes fell back deeper into his chair and tapped the edge of the paper on his lips. I dared not interrupt his thinking and left him to his own ways.

Several hours had passed since I'd heard from Holmes. From time to time, I would hear footsteps or the clang of glass jars and the striking of matches. I decided to go for an evening stroll, and just as I reached for the door handle to leave, I was stopped.

"Watson! Do not step out that door!" the voice of Holmes came shouting down the staircase. "Don't just stand there, my man, get yourself back into the study!"

I rolled my eyes, took my coat off, and ascended back into the study. Holmes was standing in the doorway with arms crossed. He had a smirk on his face as he leaned against the doorframe.

"You called me back?" I said.

"Do I detect agitation in your voice?" he asked. "Never mind, leave it be. I have made a discovery and wish to share the results with you!"

"What have you found?" I asked and followed him back into the study.

He stood at his chemical desk, set the letter down, and picked up an empty slip of paper.

"After you left me, I realised something. There was an interesting aroma to the paper. Upon closer examination, I soon found that it had been washed in a solution; a solution meant to go undetected to the untrained eye, or nose perhaps. Porlock knows me well. He surely heard of our achievements with his last message regarding Mr Douglas, so he left me to my own devices to figure it out again. The next clue was a remnant of baking soda in the envelope, which, as you may know, is often used to create invisible ink. Here is an example." Taking a slip of paper and holding it over a flame, he showed me the effects as the word 'see' appeared. "So, Watson, let us try this together with Porlock's letter," said Holmes.

I nodded, and Holmes picked up the letter. He extended it over a small flame. Slowly, the white paper began to turn yellow in places. After a few moments, a word was revealed.

HAGUE

The word came into focus, and Holmes grinned like a mischievous schoolboy.

"Hague," I read. "What's the meaning of it?"

"It matters not, Watson. Hague is the keyword. Now we can figure out the cypher." He took up his pen and wrote a table. On one row, he wrote the alphabet, and underneath, he used the keyword to figure out the cryptic alphabet, which could be used to decipher the message.

"D is a substitute for 'G', so let us see. We have a G-R-E-A-T. Great. 'U' is a 'C'. Capital! New word then, C-A-T-A-S-T-R-O-P-H-E. Two words now, 'Great Catastrophe.' 'L' is a stand-in for the letter 'M'. The 'E's are 'E's, and 'S' is a substitute for 'T'. Next word is, Meet. 'H' is an 'A', AT. Great Catastrophe - Meet At. 'K' stands in for 'L', L-I-O-N-S. 'G' is a 'D', D-E-N. 'W' is a 'W'. W-H-I-T-E. 'U' is a 'C'. C-H-A-P-E-L. There we have it, then, Watson. We broke the cypher! 'Great Catastrophe. Meet At Lions Den. Whitechapel.'" Holmes stood straight up after his victory and was silent.

"Meet at Whitechapel? When? He does not specify a time," said I.

"Perhaps he did," said Holmes. He shot over to the table next to his chair and picked up the envelope. He smelled it carefully and held it over the fire we had used with the envelope. Words began to develop across the back. When it was fully visible, it read:

TONIGHT: MIDNIGHT

"Never before has Fred Porlock wanted to meet," said Holmes.

"Perhaps it's a trap?" I suggested.

"It is quite possible that it is, my friend. But I cannot refuse this invitation. My interest has been piqued." Holmes then turned and looked at me. It was not the look of a detective, but that of a friend. "Watson, I do not want to endanger you if you wish to stay behind," and I held up my hand in immediate protest.

"Holmes, I shall not let you walk into the Lion's Den alone. I will be by your side."

"Splendid, old chap! It is reassuring to have someone with me whom I can rely on wholeheartedly, my dear friend. What is the time? Ah, nearing half-past nine, just a few more hours to wait. Rest up, dear Watson, and we will begin our trek around ten till eleven."

I rejected the idea of an evening stroll, knowing that shortly I would be rushed out into the colder night air for what looked to be a promising adventure. I allowed myself a brief nap in my room, followed by a warm cup of tea and a small shot of whisky to awaken my senses before venturing out with Holmes.

As I waited, I could hear him in his room, and at ten thirty, he burst forth dressed in a dark cloth cap and a long black coat. I put on my coat and hat, and we vacated the premises. Waiting for us outside was a hansom that Holmes had arranged for us, and we were ushered towards Whitechapel, the Lion's Den, and the mysterious Porlock.

*****

As we approached the Salvation Army, Holmes instructed the hansom driver to stop. He paid the man; then, we continued on foot. Whitechapel was not an area I acquired great pleasure from during the day, let alone at night. The deeper we ventured into the cesspool of humanity, the more I saw the people of the abyss, and I came to realise how horribly degenerate it was. Holmes took us down a small dark alleyway, hidden from the more respectable folk of our society. We carried on until we saw a small sign hanging over a narrow door. Poorly carved into the wooden sign was the name The Lion's Den. Men of a very poor nature were ushered in and out of the door, stumbling from intoxication, getting into mumbled verbal battles and sloppy fistfights.

Holmes and I pushed our way through the crowd and forcefully entered the narrow door into a dark, gloomy bar. "You will find the lowest of the low in this place. It is no surprise that someone associated with the late Professor Moriarty would choose a meeting place such as this," said Holmes as he scanned the room, evaluating our situation. I glanced around, keeping track of exits and looking for immediate threats.

"Mr Olmes," said a behemoth-like man with a Cockney accent. He was bald with beady eyes, and his face and arms were covered in scars and tattoos. Even Holmes, with his outstanding fighting capabilities, and I, with my military training, would not care to tackle this giant of a man.

"Yes, I am he."

"You'll come this way," said the man. Holmes and I nodded, and we followed the behemoth through the bar, up a small flight of stairs, through a dark hallway, and finally into a surprisingly decent, well-lit room. There was no one inside the room, but in the centre was a large table with four chairs around it. There, on the table, was an unmarked bottle of what appeared to be red wine, along with four glasses. The walls were decorated with decent-looking paintings of vast landscapes and ferocious oceanic scenery.

"Sit down. He'll be with you shortly," our guide announced while he stepped out and locked the door, trapping us inside.

"This is interesting," said Holmes.

"Terrifying is more appropriate, I reckon."

"I say we should take a seat. No, Watson, best to keep our backs to the wall and face the door," said Holmes.

I took my chair and repositioned it. We sat there for nearly a quarter of an hour, listening to the ruckus of people down below, before we heard someone fiddling with the lock. We jumped to our feet, prepared for anything to come rushing through the door. Before the handle turned, there was a loud bang and a brief yell, which was more of a loud gulp, followed by the sound of feet fleeing down the hall.

Holmes raced to the locked door and forced it open. A man fell into his arms, gasping as blood pooled at their feet. "Watson!" cried Holmes, and I darted to his aid, helping him carry the dying man and lay him gently on the table. He was coughing up blood.

Holmes tore the man's shirt off and revealed the gruesome wounds beneath. It did not take long for us to realise that we could not aid this man. Holmes grabbed the man's face, whose eyes locked with Holmes's, and he cracked a smile.

"It is good... to... see you in person," the victim said.

"You know who I am?" asked Holmes.

"Very well. I must thank you for never... attempting to find out my identity," gurgled the man.

"Are you Porlock?" Holmes asked. The man nodded. "Why did you call us here? What great danger is there?"

"Le... lega... legacy, Mr Holmes. It's all full circle."

"Be more clear, sir!" said Holmes sternly. The man tried to speak, but it was very difficult.

"There are many… strands… of the web," Porlock said with strained force. "I know… little. Yet, the plan is big. The man with… with…"

Porlock was barely hanging on to life now.

"The cross scar. May… may… Eighteen… eight… teen," Porlock's head fell back on the table, his eyes empty and staring into the void.

His soul passed as Holmes and I stood in disbelief.

He walked over to the wall and buried his face in his palm. In a very rare moment, he lashed out and slammed his fist against the wall. It was common to find him bored or agitated with stagnation, but there have been very few times when I have seen him burst out in such fierce anger. He walked back over to the lifeless body and rummaged through the pockets. He found a bloody card in the shirt pocket. Holmes rubbed some of the blood off and stared intensely at it.

"What's that?" I asked.

"Nothing," he returned. "Watson, did you hear that?" I stopped and listened, trying to single out whatever noise he had detected, but I could not hear a thing.

"Hear what? There is only silence."

"Precisely," said Holmes, and he ran out the door and looked down the hallway.

The building was silent. I followed after, and we proceeded slowly, anticipating an attack. At the bottom of the stairway, the door was shut. We attempted to open it, but it was jammed.

"We are locked in!" I said. "We must find another way out."

The next moment, we were both rattled by a tremendous explosion. The door unhinged slightly, and we could see into the bar. The entire room was in flames. There was no way we could pass through there now.

"Quick, Watson, back up the stairs!" shouted Holmes.

We ran up to find that the hallway was filling with smoke.

"Someone knew Porlock was coming here to disclose vital information and set this trap. Let's try to find a window through which we can escape."

Holmes and I kicked in the doors along the hall. Most of the rooms were ablaze and filled with black smoke, which flooded the corridor, further hindering our visibility. We kicked in the last door on the right and found it was hardly affected by the blast.

On the other side was a window with a staircase.

We walked across the floor steadily. Holmes took a step, then suddenly pushed me back as the floor gave way, and he fell through. I fell to my knees to find him hanging on to the edge.

Down below him raged a fierce fire. Smoke rushed up at us, stinging our eyes, making it hard to see.

"Steady, Holmes! Steady!" I said, grabbing his arms and heaving him back up.

Some of the supporting beams remained, and we slowly and gently balanced our way across them to the other side. We reached the window and quickly opened it. Holmes forced me through first. As I stuck my head out, someone fired two shots at me.

"That way is blocked!" said Holmes.

"I noticed!" I returned.

Holmes and I looked around the room, hoping to find some other way out. At what seemed to be the very same moment, Holmes and I spotted a hatch in the ceiling leading into an attic.

"If we can get in there, we should be able to escape through the connected building!" yelled Holmes over the crackling of the blaze.

We gingerly made our way to the side of the room where the hatch was. Holmes stood on my shoulders and pulled it open. A very weak ladder came down. The pair of us raced up the ladder into the damp and stale attic. We climbed across the beams until we reached the wall. Holmes found a narrow crawlspace, and we darted through. Finding ourselves in the building next door, we breathed a sigh of relief.

"Here, Watson!" said Holmes. "I found the exit."

Holmes forced the hatch to open, and we descended into the safety of the connecting building. There seemed to be no life in this building as Holmes and I searched for a way out. I assumed that, with the blast next door, anyone inside had certainly vacated.

Holmes said, "It would be wise to find a side exit, what with the front likely being watched, much like the back."

"I would agree."

Within a few minutes, Holmes and I found a side door that opened into a narrow alley. We darted down it unseen and towards the back of the building.

There was no one in sight, nothing. With great speed, we raced through back streets and narrow paths until we found a lonely hansom.

We startled the poor driver, but Holmes offered to pay him generously if he raced us back to Baker Street. Admittedly, I was on edge the entire journey back to our lodging and did not feel safe until we passed through

Trafalgar Square, leaving the foulness of Whitechapel behind us.

*****

"That was far too much excitement for my liking tonight," I said, lowering my feet into a basin of hot salt water. Holmes sat in his chair, smoking his pipe and fondling the card he had pulled from Porlock. "What was the point of it all, though, Holmes?" I asked.

"The only solid piece of evidence we got from him was a man with a cross scar. This is our lead," said Holmes.

"Yes, but a lead for what? We still have the Applegates' daughter to worry about," I said.

"Yes, she is still on my mind. Tomorrow we must go and see them. I hope we can reveal some clues to her whereabouts. She fits the type that the snatcher has been hunting," said Holmes. "But this is something most troublesome." He handed over a blood-stained card that he had taken from Porlock's body. I took it into my hands and ran my eyes over it. The card was thick, with a deep imprint of one word: "Peer."

"What is its meaning?" I asked.

"A name or organisation, I assume. What it leads to is, for now, out of my hands. There is a sinister game afoot," Holmes paused a moment, then added, "Watson, everything comes in full circle, and Porlock warned that there is a legacy waiting to be reckoned with."

"Whose legacy, Holmes?" I asked.

"A master villain," Holmes muttered.

"Was not Professor Moriarty the great crescendo to your work? We cannot be threatened with his return again?"

"His organisation ran deep, Watson."

"All that concluded after the Diamond Jubilee, when the MPL was disposed of, did it not?"

"All is not as it seems," said he reflectively. "Watson, get some rest, we have an early start with the Applegates tomorrow. Expect a long day, my friend." With that, Holmes spoke no more of the matter. He stood and retired to his room while I sat and mulled over the long events of the day. There was great concern on my friend's face as he left. I recalled what he had said earlier: "This was only scratching the surface of something much bigger than we expected."

The next morning, I was greeted in the study with a luscious breakfast of fried eggs, bacon, and toast. I partook of my morning meal and waited for any sign of Holmes. As I waited, I skimmed through the morning's paper. The headlines regarded the three young ladies who were found dead and the extravagant fire in Whitechapel. The paper confirmed the identities of the three women as Edith Smith, Marge Owens, and Sandra Vanders. It gave no indication of any suspects, but that the Metropolitan Police were hard at work trying to find the person, or persons, responsible. There were, however, hints that the Ripper had returned, but Inspector Reid of Division H made it clear that it was not likely.

"Interesting morning read, eh, Watson?" said Holmes, coming into the study.

"Good Lord, man, have you been out already this morning?"

"Indeed, I have, old boy. I was informing Lestrade of our night's activities."

"Very well. Care for some food?"

"Trifles, Watson. We should be off soon if we are to make our way to the Applegates' house by nine." I nodded and went to the toilet to clean up and shave, then met Holmes back in the study. He was ready, with coat and hat on. I took mine off the hanger and followed swiftly behind.

*****

We rapidly made our way to Kensington and soon found ourselves standing in front of the Applegates' house. It was a two-storey building in the middle of a long row of Georgian houses. As we walked up the steps, the front door was immediately opened by a maid, as if she had been ordered to await our arrival.

"The Applegates will see you in the study," she said as she escorted us to the room. The two of them were sitting in large brown leather-bound chairs, holding a saucer and a steaming cup of tea in what looked like incredibly fine china cups.

"Good morning, Mr Holmes. Good morning, Doctor," said the pair. Mr Applegate stood, extended his hand, and we each shook it firmly.

"Would you show me to your daughter's room, please?" said Holmes straight away.

"Would you care for anything to drink? And please, do tell us what you learnt from last night," Mr Applegate enquired.

"My findings from last night, currently, have no bearing on you, and it would be improper of me to disclose them. What would be beneficial is if you would take me to the young lady's room so I may continue my investigation." Holmes was stern with Mr Applegate, and I, myself, felt slightly annoyed at his less-than-interested attitude in letting Holmes and me carry on.

"Continue, you say. I would say you have not yet begun!" snarled Mr Applegate.

"It is of no issue to me what becomes of your daughter. If you want her found alive, I can find her. If you want her found dead, I can walk away and leave you to it. And any more of this gibberish uttered from your mouth will see my colleague and me out the door with no more say in the matter," said Holmes.

71

"Edward, please!" pleaded Mrs Applegate, her face red with embarrassment and fear.

"Accept my apologies, Mr Holmes. It is a trying time for us all," said he.

"Accepted. Please take us to her room," said Holmes.

Mr and Mrs Applegate took us up the stairs to a large open room looking out on the back garden. Passing through the door, there was a daybed to our left, a desk full of expensive perfumes to our right, a walk-in closet next to it, and a small chair and table with a book that looked regularly used in front of a large bay window.

"If you will all stand back, I need the room to myself." Holmes wandered about, examining the personal belongings. He whipped open the closet doors, pulled out his magnifying glass, and started looking at her shoes. "Interesting, would I be right that she buys clothing at Bessie's Boutique and shoes from Vanders, near Leicester Square?"

"Yes, she has often purchased items from both shops," said Mrs Applegate. Holmes then walked over to the daybed and, with a great jerk, tossed the mattress up on its side. There, underneath, was a small pile of letters. Holmes picked them up, Mrs Applegate began to push in, but I stopped her.

"Is there something you should tell us?" Holmes asked. Her face looked frightened.

"What are those? How did you know they were there? Tell me!" she said.

Holmes opened the letter and read.

"The mattress, you could see a distinct curve from frequent lifting. It indicated to me that someone was hiding something. As for these, they are letters, from what seems an admirer. Signed with the name Adrien," said Holmes.

"Explain this to me!" demanded Mr Applegate. Mrs Applegate began to shake.

"Darling, I'm sorry I kept this from you," she nervously said.

"Adrien Laurent! Is that who those letters are from?! That self-righteous French swine? That orphaned beggar who pestered our girl?!"

"He only pestered you!" she cried.

"Might you tell us where your daughter went for her holiday?" Holmes asked.

"We told you, she visited family!" roared Mr Applegate. He turned and looked at his wife, and by her expression, he could see the lie coming to the surface. "She was with family?!"

"Mrs Applegate, who was it that sent and received the wires?" said Holmes.

"It was I," she replied.

"Your daughter was never missing. She eloped with this Mr Laurent. Mr Applegate did not approve, so you let them go in secret. However, something went wrong. She still didn't return home when you thought she would. I reckon you tried to contact them and got no reply, and you covered it by saying you messaged your family. All Mr Applegate needed to know was that she was missing. And it would come as no surprise to learn that Mr Laurent is missing, too." Mrs Applegate nodded. "Mr Applegate, you say he was an orphaned beggar?"

"He is, rather, a despicable, wealthy Frenchman. He took an instant shine to my Rena, and I was not in agreement with this relationship. He was taking up all her time, keeping her away from her social duties, so I stepped in and told him to leave her and our family alone. That was the last I heard of him. Though now I wonder if she even continued with her social duties!"

"I can assume she did not. Will you confirm this, Mrs Applegate?"

"That is partly true. She would go and make appearances where needed, then they would meet. I saw no real reason to keep them apart. She loved him…"

"She did not love him!" interrupted Mr Applegate.

"She did, Edward, but you ignored it!"

"It would be wise if you would tell me about this Adrien Laurent," pressed Holmes.

"Fine. But I need a strong drink! We can continue this downstairs." Holmes and I followed the couple back into the study, where Mr Applegate poured himself a rather tall glass of whisky and then took a seat.

"Best if you start, Martha," he said, taking a large gulp of his whisky. She nodded and looked up at Holmes and me as we sat across from them.

"Well, Mr Laurent, as said, was from France. He came to London last year. We met him at a dinner at Lord Joseph Jenkins's house. He was very well travelled and entertained us with extravagant stories from his ventures. All the women took a quick shine to him. He was dashing and rich; a young woman's dream. Many of the mothers were eyeing him in hopes of passing off their daughters to him. But his eye shone for our daughter from the start. I remember he commented on her hair, saying it was the most beautiful blonde hair he'd ever seen."

"He was obsessed with it," scoffed Mr Applegate, "Laurent was a predator, stalking new prey, nothing more."

"Tell me, what did he look like?" asked Holmes.

"A rough bag," Mr Applegate remarked.

"He was tall, maybe six feet. Dark brown hair and blue eyes. He was never completely clean-shaven. He had a few scars, one of which was a large crucifix-shaped one on his arm."

"A crucifix, you say?" said Holmes. Mrs Applegate nodded. "Did Mr Laurent ever tell you where he lived?"

"No, but Rena mentioned he lived in a conservative apartment at 27 Litchfield Street, off Charing Cross Road," said Mrs Applegate.

"Did you ever visit, or did Rena?"

"No, we never did, nor did she, to my knowledge. He was keen on his privacy."

"Thank you. This has been enlightening," said Holmes. "And where did they go to elope?" Mr Applegate turned and looked at his deceiving wife, awaiting the answer. "They really did go to Bristol. They stayed in a cottage by the sea called Bay Side. All the arrangements were made well in advance. They had a quick service at the court and took a train straight after."

Mr Applegate was as red as a cherry when he heard his wife speak of these matters.

"I think we shall leave you now. I will follow these leads. Thank you, both," said Holmes, standing up. "I will see what I can find on Mr Laurent. His disappearance might be the key to unlocking your daughter's disappearance. And perhaps you will have learnt a lesson, Mrs Applegate, some secrets can have deadly and devastating outcomes," Holmes finished. She held her head low, and Mr Applegate showed us to the door.

Holmes sat with legs and arms crossed as the hansom moved over the cobbled roads. By the look on his face, I could see he was in deep thought.

"This woman was in over her head!" said he.

"Rena?" I asked.

"No, the mother! She must have known her actions would have drastic results." Holmes tapped to get the hansom driver's attention. "My man, please take us to Scotland Yard."

"What are we doing there?" I asked but received no return.

*****

Upon arrival at Scotland Yard, Holmes spoke with Lestrade, informing him of the events at the Applegate house, and asked for any information on Adrien Laurent.

"Holmes, I have no record of a man by that name. I'm trying to acquire the name of the person who owns the building at Linchfield. Perhaps they could be of use to us."

"Lestrade, I am uneasy about this case. I believe whoever took Miss Rena Applegate is responsible for the murders of those three women," said Holmes.

"How can you be so sure?" Lestrade asked.

"The three young women are fitting a mould. Early twenties, wealthy background, and all have blonde hair," said Holmes.

"Do you suppose this kidnapper killed Laurent?" Lestrade asked.

"If the situation called for it, this kidnapper does not seem opposed to killing." As Holmes finished, an officer walked in and handed Lestrade a slip of paper.

"There we are. We have a name, Jeremiah Daniels. He owns the building and rents out the apartments. Seems like a good lead to follow. Maybe he can shed some light on Laurent's disappearance," said Lestrade.

"This is interesting!" said Holmes excitedly. "Watson and I will go see what we can find. Ah, Lestrade. What did you learn of Mrs James, the boutique shop owner; did her alibi hold?"

"It did. She was at the theatre with her husband," said Lestrade, and Holmes nodded slowly. "I'm going to get someone onto this Daniels right away," said Lestrade.

"No! Postpone any serious police involvement. Give me some time to gather more data," recommended Holmes sharply.

"This is serious, Holmes! We have two missing persons. We cannot let it rest," said Lestrade.

"I am in no way suggesting that we leave it rest. I am not in the business of rest, Lestrade. All I am asking is that you let me see what I can discover first, then pass it over to you," he returned, Lestrade's face looking perturbed. "Tell me a time when I let you down? You know very well that even when I carry on with my own path, I reach the correct conclusion, and most times even before the authorities."

Lestrade stood there looking at Holmes, whose eyes were burning.

"You've got until tomorrow. Then we have to step in," said Lestrade.

"Come, Watson, the game is afoot!"

What Became of Rena Applegate

We arrived at 27 Linchfield to find no one answering the door.

"We should find a back door," said Holmes. "The alley, this way, should prove fruitful."

Once around the back, Holmes quickly picked the lock, and we found ourselves inside. The windows were covered with heavy, thick curtains which blacked out the room almost entirely. I opened the curtains covering the back windows so as not to cause any movement on the main road that might catch someone's attention. Holmes held a torch, and we searched the house. We shifted through the cabinets and drawers. I heard Holmes mumbling to himself, but he did not disclose anything.

"An oil lamp, and the glass is still warm," he whispered. "Someone has been here recently."

As we continued to look around, it was apparent that this house was owned by someone of great wealth. Expensive paintings hung on the walls, and a crystal chandelier hung from the ceiling. Priceless vases and relics from East Asia, Africa, the Americas, and mainland Europe were scattered throughout the rooms.

"Whoever this Laurent man is, he is most certainly well travelled," said I.

We came to a closed door, and Holmes asked me to get my revolver out. I took my position as he slowly opened the door.

There was no one inside. The room we found ourselves in was truly an unusual bedroom. There was an oil lamp next to me, and I lit it to help light up this dark area. We found that the windows were completely boarded up and nailed shut.

Nothing could get in or out save through the single door. There were hundreds of half-burnt candles and wax spots all over the tables and floor. There was a large bed in the middle, with chains and cuffs hanging down from the canopy. Holmes opened the closet, and what we found was most interesting. In the closet was an arsenal of costumes, only fit for a woman, and several long blonde-haired wigs of various styles.

"Who do you think these all belong to?" I asked.

"I am not sure, Watson," he returned. There was a deep chest on the floor, and Holmes pulled it out of the closet and into the room. He flung the top open, and inside was a large pile of women's clothing and several pairs of shoes. Four pairs of shoes and dresses, to be exact. One of the shoes was Vanders' make. "I have been slow, Watson, so very slow!" he paused. "This is no one's lodging. This place has a more sinister use."

"What do you mean?" said I.

"Observe, Watson, the wigs, the costumes, the bed, the blacked-out windows, and the copious amounts of female clothing indicate the room's true nature. Further, this chest, the clothes inside are well made and expensive, but not to the standard of those in the closet, same with the shoes. The girls who wore these were forced to take them off and put on something else. Watson, this place is a brothel, and no ordinary one."

Suddenly, something caught Holmes's attention. He paused and was silent.

"What is it?" I asked.

"Do you hear that, Watson?"

"Afraid not."

"That, that tapping?" I stood still, trying to ignore the racing thud of my heart to listen to what Holmes was hearing. Then I heard it: a small thumping sound.

"Is it someone outside? Some workers, perhaps?"

"I should think not. That is inside the house." Holmes dashed out of the room, moving like a cat through the house, looking for the origin of the sound. In the lounge, he put his head into the fireplace, pulled it out, and looked around the mantel. Then, he began feeling his way along the wall to the right. He knocked on random parts of the wall, then pressed his ear against it. He took a step back and reclined on the large oak sofa that sat in front of the fireplace. "What do you notice, Watson?" he asked.

"I'm not sure," I paused, "the noise is gone."

"Well, yes, it is, but what else?" he pressed. I walked over to the wall and tapped as he had. The part of the wall I tapped was firm, like hitting bricks, until I moved a few more paces over, and the knocks suddenly felt hollow. "It would seem there's a large hole behind this wall!" I ejaculated. Holmes then stood up and walked to the mantel.

"Six gold hooks, all remarkably shiny. Apart from one," said he, pulling on it. I then felt a release of air as the wall before me popped open, revealing a hidden door.

"The less shiny hook was faded from constant use!" I cried.

"Indeed," said Holmes.

As we opened the door, we saw a long, dark staircase going deep below the house. Holmes pulled out his torch, and we descended. When we reached the bottom of this dark and cold cellar, we could neither see nor hear anything.

Looking around, the walls were riddled with rusty chains and cuffs, all their uses far too horrible to imagine. The cellar seemed to follow the layout of the house above. As we turned to shine the light into the black void of a room, we both took fright to see a young woman with blonde hair.

She was dressed in only a frail undergarment, chained, gagged, and bruised, lying on the floor. I raced over to her. When I did, her eyes opened, and she kicked me in the face.

"Calm yourself, woman, we are here to help you!" Holmes's voice echoed as she fought violently with the chains to keep her distance from us. "Be calm, Rena. All will be well," he assured her again. At the sound of her name, she began to calm down, and her frantic breathing subsided. I walked over and took the gag out of her mouth. Her eyes were red and her face stained with tears.

"Please... please help me!" she cried.

"You are Rena Applegate?" Holmes asked.

"Yes, yes, I am!" she stammered.

"Let us get you out of here. We need to speak with you at length before anything else can be done." Holmes worked on the locks and popped both clasps around her wrists. He picked the poor girl up and took her out the back door. Holmes and I made sure we left the house in the same order that we found it, so as not to signal our entry. We waved a hansom that took us back to Baker Street.

*****

Once at Baker Street, we left the young woman to clean up and rest. Mrs Hudson brought up some soup and tea for the miss, and after she had eaten, Holmes took to asking her questions.

"Miss Rena, your parents hired me to help find you. We know of your relationship with Mr Laurent. What has become of him? Is he alive?" Holmes asked.

"Alive? Yes, that man is very much alive!" she said with great hatred in her voice. "Mr Holmes, he is the one who did this! That man, that horrible demon. He was so elegant at first. So gentle and persuasive! My father did not approve of him, but he was so kind, so wealthy. I would have been a fool to pass up the chance of marrying a man like that, yet diving in so deep so quickly was indeed the foolish thing. It was everything he wanted, and in the end, he was nothing more than a predator!"

She rose from her seat and paced the study.

"We… we married and went to the train station to leave for a honeymoon," Rena continued. "When we got there, he said he had left something and that we needed to go get it. He took me to a boutique shop on Aldgate High Street, Bessie's Boutique is the name. He said he had bought me a dress and wanted me to wear it. He demanded I try it on, so I did. I tried it on in the shop according to his request. When I put it on, he turned into an animal. He lunged at me and demanded intercourse," she paused a moment, putting her hand over her quivering mouth. "I told him no and to wait, but it wasn't good enough. There, in the shop, amidst my screams and pleas, he raped me. It was such a horrible feeling being raped by someone you… loved," she began to cry for several moments. Fighting back the tears, she continued.

"Afterwards, I heard him thank the shopkeeper, who said she'd have more clothes for him soon and that someone was inquiring about a night's service. He then took me back to his house where he kept me hidden in the cellar and only pulled me out when he wanted me… or had sold me!

"It was in there that I discovered I was not the only one he had tricked. When he forced me into the cellar, there were three other women in there. They told me that he had tricked them all too, and that he used them for some perverted sex trade. He would bring women back, horrible, nasty women from the street. They would wear the clothes and the wigs for him, and he'd force one of us to come join them.

"He did more than just sell our bodies to high-paying fiends. He would often sell a girl to the foreign sex trade. One girl was rumoured to be sold to some military figure in Europe. One day, the other three girls kicked up a fuss, thinking that we could overpower him, but failed. He said that if they did not shut up, he'd cut their hair off and slash them open. Nevertheless, they didn't stop, so he drugged them, and that was the last I saw of those three."

"Did you get their names?" Holmes asked.

"Yes, one was Edith Smith, another was Mage, no, Marge. I cannot recall her last name. The other was Sandra Vanders. I remember her because her father owns the shoe shop," said Miss Applegate.

"Yes, we found their bodies," said Holmes. Miss Applegate's shoulders heaved at hearing this statement. Her body shook, though her eyes seemed void, like her spirit had just been snuffed out.

"Where is Mr Laurent now?" I asked.

"If Laurent is in fact his real name," said Holmes.

"I'm not sure, but the owner of the boutique called him Dez." When Miss Applegate mentioned that, Holmes stood up. He wandered over to a pile of papers, pulled some out, and took a seat.

"Watson, the other girls were marked with a 'Z'. Do you remember? Several years ago, in Poland, a young woman, blonde-haired no less, went missing. When she was found, she was barely alive, her hair in tatters, and she was marked with a 'Z' burned into her thigh, just like these girls. She called the man 'Dez' in the reports, and she said he spoke with a French accent. Laurent could be the very same man as her kidnapper, who was never caught. And you know just as well as I do, Watson, it is easy to get lost in this jungle. We must find him and stop his reign of terror," said Holmes. "Miss Rena, what more can you tell us?"

"Laurent did come back after he took the girls. He said if I didn't obey, I would end up like them. I honestly didn't know if death would be better than to suffer any more of this," she paused while tears filled her eyes and ran down her cheek. "I wasn't sure, Mr Holmes, I just wasn't sure." Miss Applegate sat unashamedly, allowing her tears to wet her blouse. "I mean, I wasn't sure if he had really killed the others. Deep within, I felt he had killed them, and yet… I did allow a flicker of hope within my heart that he was just trying to keep me in line."

We then heard the loud bang of a door closing, and Mrs Hudson yelling at someone to stop, insisting that Mr Holmes was busy. Our study room door flew open, and in rushed Mrs Applegate.

"Mr Holmes, I saw him! I saw Mr Laurent, I tried to catch him, but he slipped away!"

Then she paused. She saw her child sitting there at our table.

"Rena! I'm sorry, I am so sorry!" cried Mrs Applegate. Her eyes welled up, and both mother and daughter dove into each other's arms.

"It is over now, mother, it's all over. I love you," her daughter said in comfort.

"What happened, where is Laurent?" asked Mrs Applegate.

"Mother, this was all his doing. He took me, he fooled us all!" cried Miss Rena. The two held each other for some time before Holmes interrupted.

"Good ladies, we have a window, a rare opportunity to catch this villainous swine before he slips through our fingers. If you are up to it, Miss Applegate, and if we are not too late, we could see this end tonight."

"What do you want?" she asked.

"Mr Holmes! My dear Rena has been through enough. I cannot allow you to use her as a pawn in some insane game to trap this hideous man," said Mrs Applegate.

"Mother, this is my choice to make. You have no idea what he did. I want to see this man stopped," said Rena Applegate. "Mr Holmes, what's your plan?"

*****

Holmes's plan was less than enthralling from my end. He needed a distraction, so he put me in a quick disguise and sent me off to the boutique to enquire about the hiring of a lady. While I was there, Holmes and Miss Rena returned to her house of torture at 27 Linchfield. It cannot go without saying that my admiration for this woman grew, seeing her willingness to step back into the devil's lair to bring him to justice. She certainly possessed a rare power that most women do not have. I found my way to the boutique on Aldgate High Street, and when I stepped inside, a little bell chimed. Moments later, I was greeted by Mrs Bessie James.

"How can I help you?" she asked.

"I am here to enquire about your services," said I, attempting to mask my voice to fit my disguise.

"Are you looking for a dress for your lady?" she asked.

"I am looking for the lady rather than the dress," said I. My stomach churned at the words coming from my mouth. I did not understand how any sober man could request a service of this nature. Mrs James looked at me for some moments.

"What are you looking for?" she asked.

"A blonde," said I.

"How much do you have?" she asked. I showed her my wallet, which seemed to satisfy her. "Let me make a call," she said, and walked away. I heard her speaking to someone by way of telephone before she came back. "Mr Dezmond will be here soon and show you to your mistress."

I waited for half an hour before this Mr Dezmond arrived. He was tall, had dark hair and blue eyes. He was in need of a shave and had several scars. When I shook his hand, his sleeve went up and revealed a crucifix-style marking on his arm. He fitted, exactly, the description of Mr Adrien Laurent.

"Good to meet you, I am Mr Dezmond," said he in a sharp French accent. "Sorry for being late, Monsieur. I have been running around all day. Never a day when someone does not try to stop you in the streets. And your name, monsieur?"

"James Smith," said I.

"Smith, eh?" said Mr Dezmond with a grin. "Well, it makes no difference to me if you hide your name, as long as you pay, I am happy!"

"Then we are set," said I, handing him the money. He took it and counted it. When he was pleased, he asked me to follow him, and we left the boutique and took a hansom to 27 Linchfield. The ride to the house was one of the most dreadful experiences I have had in my time with Holmes. Knowing full well what this madman had done and was doing, while forcing myself to pretend to be of his breed, was gut-wrenching.

"So, you are looking for a blonde, eh? Well, even if I didn't have a blonde, we have all the right equipment to make my girls suit your style. However, you are in luck, I recently came across a truly outstanding blonde. If I am ever strapped for money, I know she will sell for a very generous sum!" Mr Dezmond exclaimed with a curling smile.

"Yes, indeed! Not a bad wild card to play, I'd say," I remarked.

"No, it is not. Yes, she'll do you just fine, I think," said Dezmond slimily.

Soon, we approached the house. We stepped inside, and he took me to the bedroom that Holmes and I had previously rummaged through. Dezmond pulled out a drawer full of images of women in various scandalous outfits. "Now, Mr Smith, you pick the outfit of your choice, and I'll take it down to her to get changed into," said Dezmond. Without caring to look, I put my finger down on an image. "Ah, a man who knows what he wants. I like that." He opened the closet and found the garment. He ordered me to stay in the room, and if I did not, then the deal would be off and I'd lose the money.

Dezmond dismissed himself, and I heard him open the hatch. I poked my head out of the door and saw him descend. Moments later, I heard several feet walking up the steps, and Dezmond reappeared at the door, holding Miss Rena Applegate. He unlocked her cuffs and pushed her into the room. She walked over to me, and I looked over at Dezmond. "She's a beauty, is she not?" he said.

"Yes, and one you will not be harming any longer!" came the voice of Holmes from up the wall where he hid. I then pulled out my revolver and aimed it at Dezmond. His face was in utter shock and disbelief.

"What is this? Who are you?" roared Dezmond.

"I am Mr Sherlock Holmes, and this is my colleague. We are putting you under arrest for the kidnapping of Miss Rena Applegate and the murders of Edith Smith, Marge Owens, and Sandra Vanders." I could hear Holmes's footsteps approaching us.

Suddenly, Dezmond heaved the cuffs down the hall towards Holmes and grabbed the door handle, shutting Miss Rena and me inside. We dashed over to the door and opened it. Holmes was racing past, and Dezmond was running out the front door, but he did not have far to go. I quickly gave Miss Rena my coat for her decency as we too followed after Holmes and Dezmond.

When Dezmond exited his house, he found a host of police officers, led by Inspector Lestrade, waiting for him. Holmes, Miss Rena, and I watched him standing there, looking out in horror as his scheme crashed down at his feet. He turned and saw us blocking his back, then he reached into his coat and pulled out a revolver. Many shouts from the officers went up, ordering him to put it down, and then Dezmond shot himself in the head. His body fell and rolled down the steps onto the pavement. The police raced over to the body, and I, too, came to inspect it.

"He took the coward's way out," said Lestrade.

"He will answer for his sins one way or another," said I.

"Indeed. Never mind, though, we got his accomplice, Mrs James, at the boutique after you left with him," said Lestrade.

"Thank you, Mr Holmes and Doctor Watson. Thank you for saving me," said Miss Rena.

"Thank you for being so bold, Miss," said Holmes. We left her with Lestrade, as he needed her for questioning, and we returned to our lodgings at 221b to see the case closed.

*****

The following day, the papers were full of the story about how the police had caught the criminal responsible for the kidnappings and murders, and how he killed himself before they could apprehend him.

"Does it not bother you, Holmes, that they take all the credit even still?" I asked as we ate our breakfast.

"It does not, Watson. For most, it would, but I am not troubled by it. What I am bothered by is the missing pieces of the case."

"What missing pieces, Holmes?"

"Porlock, Watson, he warned us about the man with a cross scar before he died. Was it pure coincidence that 'Adrien Laurent', or rather 'Dezmond', had a scar on his arm in the shape of a crucifix?" Holmes paused a moment and looked right at me.

"Well, no, I guess not. What do you suppose it means?" I asked.

"Dezmond was a part of something much bigger and much deeper than we were able to uncover. While you were talking with Lestrade, I pulled this off the man's body," said Holmes. In his hand was a small white card. "There is a strange game afoot, Watson, a cold wind has started to pass through, and we should be ready for whatever storm comes our way."

"It says, Peer! It's just like the card found on Porlock," said I.

"Indeed! So who or what is Peer? Watson, perhaps in time, I will find out," said Holmes.

A STUDY IN STONE

The Sudden Death of Ronald Lovett

It was April of 1899. Holmes's iron constitution had been loosened of late. The strain of his cases had taken a severe toll on my friend's health. I pleaded with him to take a break.

"What can be gained from a holiday, Watson?! There is a furious storm brewing within the city. My mind races over the Dabish case; what purpose was he serving? Porlock, Watson, he knew something of grand proportion was at work, something beyond Mr Laurent's horrid business. Furthermore, I am no closer to discovering what Peer is! My mind is burning with questions, and yet no answers are coming! Leaving the city now will only let matters that I am widely unclear on worsen without hesitation," Holmes protested with his knees tucked under his chin. He turned his gaze to the floor. His eyes were bloodshot, and his face was painfully thin.

"Holmes! You have been poring over microscopic information. You hardly sleep, and I have not seen you eat for weeks."

"I eat when it is only of great necessity," he replied, looking back up at me.

"This will not do! As your friend and doctor, I plead with you to take a short break. Ten days at most," I tried to barter. Holmes, still sitting, turned his eyes away from me as I stood with arms crossed and concern on my face. I noticed he was looking down at the morning paper, skimming the front page.

"Look, Watson, war! It is most certainly brewing, but who is stirring the pot!? Germany points at Russia, Russia at Germany, and both point at Britain. And this! 'Calls for a Peace Summit to Discuss War Ethics.' Disgraceful, Watson.

There are no ethics in war. No, there are too many things in play to just leave."

"Holmes, please pay attention!" I begged. "You have to take a rest for your mental well-being, and for mine!" Holmes put his hands together and looked around the room for several moments before fixing his eyes on me.

"My friend, I can see you are only looking out for my best interests. Your care is deeply moving," said he, with what felt like genuine appreciation in his voice. "I will take your medical advice, and we shall take a holiday. But let us go somewhere new."

"Very well, what place strikes your fancy?" I asked, relieved that Holmes had agreed to a break.

"There is a small village in Wales called Morfa Nefyn, which rests on the beach. The sea air should do the trick for me."

"Splendid, Holmes, I shall arrange it then."

*****

A day later, Holmes and I found ourselves on a train for Wales; I had speedily made all the arrangements for us and acquired a small cottage a short walk from the beach. Our retreat from the city could not have come at a more suitable time, as clouds had begun to consume London, and a vengeful rainfall drove individuals off the cobbled streets while the roads were only shy of becoming muddy bogs. Holmes and I sat in our carriage and watched the world turn from a great metropolis to lush green farmlands and rolling hills speckled with sheep, which looked like tiny white puffs skirting across the fields.

"Thank you for agreeing to this short break, Holmes," said I.

"What will be, will be, Watson. As hard as I try, I cannot be there to head off every disaster that befalls."

"Your strands will be there for you to follow when you return," I replied. Holmes looked slightly agitated at this remark. "What I meant to say is that you need this break, and, knowing your remarkable mind, it will not take you long to recover from any momentary pause in your work."

"I can see many things at work, things that Scotland Yard cannot see for whatever juvenile reason. London is being consumed by a thick fog, Watson. A fog that, if not watched, will grow beyond restraint," said Holmes. "There are shapes which can be seen moving, sinister shapes, but you must look hard to see them, and Scotland Yard is not looking hard whatsoever."

"Let the city take care of itself these next ten days, Holmes. I, too, plan to take advantage of this holiday," said I.

"Very well, Watson," said Holmes.

He pulled his hat over his face, and whether he slept or just sat with eyes closed, I do not know, but I found it best to leave him to his own thoughts. I then leaned back myself and closed my own eyes.

The next time I opened them, we had arrived at our destination. Holmes and I unloaded our bags and reloaded them into a cart, which took us to Glan-y-mor Cottage. Once settled in, I retired to bed and left Holmes in the lounge, where he sat smoking his pipe before a warm fire.

*****

94

The next morning, I awoke and prepared for the day. Around eleven o'clock, I found a note by the door, left by Holmes, informing me that he had wandered out for a morning stroll. Following his lead, I decided to go for a walk myself. I dressed in rubber boots, a warm jacket, and a hat. I followed a small dirt path for some time.

I passed a small cottage which rested just before a beautiful natural tunnel of overhanging tree branches and vines. It was a marvel to behold as I walked through it. Within a few minutes of exiting the tunnel, I found myself looking out over the vast, deep blue ocean from the height of a cliff face. The bay was a splendid and lovely scene.

In the distance, I could see a few structures which rested on the beach itself, with large stone barricades that served as walls to keep the ocean at bay. There was also a small public house, which struck me as the type of place where many of the local fishermen would be found. Looking directly below, I saw that the tide had begun to withdraw, and not far off, I could see a tall, thin figure, feet planted deeply in the wet sand, looking out into the ocean as the waves leapt up and tripped over themselves, crashing on the shore.

I followed the small cliffside trail until its end, which sent me down a steep rock staircase to level ground. Approaching the beach, the figure turned out to be Holmes.

"Morning, Watson," said he without even turning around.

"You truly do have eyes in the back of your head!" I said.

"If only, but I saw you on the cliff when you stepped out from the footpath. More than anything, it was an educated guess that it would be you, given that I have not seen a soul walk the beach all morning."

95

"How long have you been here?"

"I began my venture around seven o'clock. I passed through a couple of tall-grass fields until I came to a ridged edge and walked along that, which took me around that hill and down here to the beach. I even spotted several seals lying on the rocks."

"Then you have had a relaxing day thus far?"

"Yes, I must commend you, Watson. This break has been most wise, and well deserved, and if I am not deceived, I think we can find us a hearty meal at that inn there," said Holmes, pointing at the stone building, its door open and smoke rising from its chimney.

"Let's go then," said I.

We proceeded towards the inn, the mixed smell of sausage, bacon, and fried fish looming in the air the closer we got.

Once inside, we were greeted by several friendly faces. The man behind the bar gave us each a pint of ale before we placed an order for food. An aged woman soon brought us a plate of golden fish and chips, each with a side of tartar sauce.

"These fish were caught here just yesterday. Fresh as can be," she said with a smile that was missing one tooth, and then left us.

"What a charming place, Holmes," said I, splashing some vinegar on my plate before cutting into the thick, battered fish.

While we consumed our food, two tall, dark-haired Welshmen entered the establishment.

"I've just been by the Lovett estate," said one of the men. "There's been murder! It was Ronald."

"What?" his friend said.

"I hear the authorities are on their way. Some kind of brawl in the night," said the first man.

"Can't say I'm much surprised! Ronald Lovett was always getting into bad situations."

"Wouldn't be surprised if it was his brother, Ralph. He's been on a short fuse the past while. Perhaps he's snapped."

"That family sure has been through a lot recently, with the engagement of Ronald's son, Randall, being broken off to that lovely Miss Stonewall. They all seem a bit out of control," and as the man finished his comment, a younger man, looking the age of seventeen years, raced inside.

I looked over at Holmes, who was no longer eating but leaning back in his chair, observing the men's conversation.

"Holmes, you leave it be," said I, but he failed to acknowledge my words.

"Excuse me, gentlemen," said Holmes.

The two Welshmen looked him over.

"Where is the Lovett estate? As it were, I am a consulting detective, and my services might be of use."

"What's your name?" one of the men asked.

"Sherlock Holmes."

The man's face lit. "Sherlock Holmes! I've heard about you. Blimey! You're here just in time then. This is a case for you, I bet! The old Principal Lovett, he's been clobbered to death in the night and there ain't no… isn't any idea who done him in," said the man. "The house is just up the road, 'bout a ten-minute walk from here. I bet they could use your help!"

"Perhaps, if the local authorities are not offended, I will make my way and offer some advice," said Holmes.

"I can't imagine they would be offended. I reckon you'd be first on the scene, though. We only heard about this early this morning, and it always takes a while before the authorities can make their way here," said the young man.

Holmes looked over at me, and he could see the aggravation on my face.

"Fear not, Watson, it cannot hurt to have a little look into the matter. As I said, the sea air has already done wonders for me," he concluded.

I nodded reluctantly at Holmes, knowing that it mattered not what I said. His mind was made up, and there was little that could distract his attention now. Holmes acquired the directions for the Lovett estate, and with that, we were off.

*****

Within ten minutes, we were walking up a path to a large estate. There was no sign of any local authorities. Even the house itself looked empty and lifeless. I knocked three times, and we waited for a response. Holmes leaned into the door. "I can hear someone coming," said he. The door opened, and there stood a short man, bald on the crown of his head with white hair hanging on the sides. His nose was rather large, and resting upon it was a pair of circular glasses. "Hello, how may I help you?" he asked.

"I am Mr Sherlock Holmes, a detective from London, and this is my colleague, Dr John Watson. I heard there was an incident in the night and wanted to offer my services."

"We do not need interference from some big name from London into our affairs. Our local order will do us fine," echoed the voice of a man from inside the house.

"And who, might you be?" I asked.

"I am Professor Ralph Lovett. It was my brother Ronald who was killed," he replied, stopping in front of the entrance to look at us.

"And my father," said another voice from behind. "I would be happy for you, Mr Holmes, to aid us in our case," said a young man, approaching us and tucking a cane into his arm to shake our hands. "I am Randall Lovett. Ronald was my father," said he. He had thick curly hair and a thin face and frame so that his clothes looked almost as if they were draped over a skeleton. Professor Ralph Lovett gave us an intense, agitated look.

"Well, I can't very well go and ignore the wishes of my dead brother's son now, can I?" said Professor Lovett, and we were shown into the house.

"Would you please show me to the scene?" Holmes asked.

"Uncle, I am not up for seeing the sight again. Might you take them?" asked young Randall. The man nodded, and we followed him through the house and out into the back garden.

"Do you all reside on the estate?" I asked.

"Our family has owned this estate for three hundred years. It is equally owned by me and my brother, which, I suppose, means me and my nephew now. We often retire here for extended periods. However, last year my brother and I decided that it would be wise to take a sabbatical from our academic responsibilities to mend our relationship. It had become strained throughout the years, so we have all been living here for the past six months. I will not deny that it has not been the easiest of times for myself," Professor Lovett admitted.

"What caused this great strain between you and your brother?" Holmes asked as we continued walking through the back garden towards a glasshouse.

"We have never got on well, ever since we were small children. I'm older, but he always fought me for leadership. Anything I did, he would go and do, trying to outshine me. He succeeded a fair number of times. More recently, I was up for the role of principal at Hawks College, a partner school with Oxford University, where he and I were both well-regarded senior lecturers. When he discovered that I was considering the change in roles, Ronald forced his way in and charmed the right people to put his name on top of the list. Mr Holmes, I cannot say I am grieving this loss. I feel whatever mess Ronald tangled himself up in, he deserved what fate had in store."

I looked over at Holmes, who did not catch my gaze but remained focused on the Professor. I could see in Ralph's eyes that he had great resentment built up towards his brother, Ronald. His anger was nothing hidden.

"Well, this is it," continued Professor Lovett as we approached a wondrous glass garden house.

The roof was entirely see-through, and the walls were lined with large open windows. I could see a staircase and a hatch with a telescope poking out. "I am a great fan of astronomy, Mr Holmes, so I had this built to contain all my equipment. Each of us used this building for our own purposes, though. It was here where I found my brother earlier this morning."

He opened the door and showed us inside. On the floor lay a silver tray and a shattered teacup. Just out of reach of the cup was a hand that belonged to the body of Ronald Lovett, who was lying on the floor in a pool of blood. There were clear signs of blunt force trauma to Ronald Lovett's head. It had been severely beaten by a blunt instrument to the point where his face was hardly recognisable. Lying across the body was a black cane covered in a Celtic design. Its handle was silver, curved, and engraved with a pattern similar to that of the stick. The cane itself was covered in blood from the victim. Holmes walked in circles around the dead body, while Professor Lovett and I observed.

"This cane was his, was it not?" Holmes asked.

"Yes, it was," replied Professor Lovett.

"Watson, what do you make of this?" asked Holmes, and I began to examine the body.

"He certainly sustained tremendous repeated blows to the head, looking at the way his frontal bone has caved in. I reckon that this was the murder weapon, too," I pointed to the cane. "You can see a fair amount of residue on the handle from the blows."

"Watson, well done!" rejoiced Holmes. "But you missed something important. He was attacked from the front." Holmes then turned to Professor Lovett, who was standing over us. "Was there no indication of a break-in?"

"None at all," he replied. Holmes walked around the room, inspecting the windows for any sign of an intruder.

"Was your brother expecting anyone?"

"No one to my knowledge, though I do not care to know who he spent his time with," remarked Professor Lovett.

"It seems transparent that your brother was not one to shy away from difficult crowds. It also appears you, too, have fierce reservations with whom your brother associates," said I.

"That is true, Doctor. It was one of our many points of disagreement. I reckon this entire mess is a result of some shadowy affair he was participating in," Professor Lovett speculated. Holmes swiftly moved through the room and stepped back outside. He fell to the ground and lay flat on his stomach for a moment, putting the grass at eye level. "What is he doing?" Professor Lovett asked.

"Looking for tracks," said Holmes, standing and crawling periodically. He circled the entire structure and came back to us. "I cannot find any unique signs of a third party that may have sneaked in. All tracks lead back and forth from here to the house," he concluded.

"Do you know who the last person to see your brother alive was?" I asked.

"I'm not sure. It might have been me," Professor Lovett said.

"What do you mean?" I asked.

"We had a conversation out here around nine o'clock last night. If anyone saw him after I did, I am not aware of it."

"Might I have a look around the house?" Holmes asked. "It would be good to look through the rooms for any clues."

"That is no trouble. Follow me."

Holmes was let loose in the manor. He left Professor Lovett and me in the dining room, where the butler, Mr Oswald, brought us a cup of tea. Professor Lovett invited him to sit with us, as there was no need to carry on with the daily duties until this matter was settled. He did not wish to; he felt it best to keep moving.

When nearly an hour had passed, Holmes returned to us.

"I have been unable to find anything of use. There was no sign that the late Ronald had an appointment of any kind; nor could I see in his ledger any great loss of money, though he probably had a separate one to keep track of his gambling escapades. Our next step, Professor Lovett, is to speak with the others in the house to reconstruct a detailed account of the events leading up to this crime. Could you provide an adequate space to conduct several interviews?"

"I can arrange that, yes. You can use the study, come with me."

Holmes and I followed the Professor into a large study. The walls were lined with shelves from top to bottom. Every inch of them was filled with large leather-bound books, some of which looked very old. Professor Lovett asked Mr Oswald to call for young Randall, who had been in his room the entire time. Once all were assembled, Mr Oswald and Randall were told to wait outside to be called in later.

What Happened The Night Before

Holmes and I took a seat opposite Professor Lovett.

"Tell me your events of the day," Holmes pressed.

He thought for a moment. "I spent a large portion of my day out on the sea," said the Professor. "We own a small boat that, on occasion, I sail along the coast. I must have been up at around five o'clock and on the water by seven. I saw no one and assumed no one saw me. I was up well before the butler, so I packed myself a lunch and took some reading materials with me. I did not return to shore until three o'clock that afternoon. I recall several walkers seeing me and waving while I rowed later in the day, though I was too far out to make any notice as to who they were. Even if I were close enough, I still may not have known them. Unlike my nephew and brother, I have not cared to invest my time in the locals. They know me, but I do not know them. Only a handful do I know by name. Upon returning to shore, I walked the beach, but not without stopping for a drink at the inn. You can speak with the keeper there. He can confirm this. I left the inn after a few drinks, returned to the estate, washed up, and ate supper with my brother and nephew. I believe the meal lasted until eight o'clock."

"What mood was your brother, Ronald, in that night?" Holmes queried.

"There was nothing unusual about his demeanour, if that is what you mean. He was his arrogant self, as always. He was boasting heavily, all night, about the incredible changes he'd made since taking on his new role as Principal. I stomached all I could and dismissed myself. An hour later, after I had calmed down, I wished to use my telescope when I saw that it was a clear night. When I entered the garden house, I found my brother inside. He smelt strongly of alcohol, and his mood was less than appealing. I attempted to get my telescope ready, but all he could do was ramble on about his job and, in a patronising way, commend my own role at the University. I very quickly lost the desire to gaze at the stars and retired to my room, where I stayed the rest of the night."

"What more can you tell me of your brother's habits and the crowds he frequented?" Holmes pressed.

"My brother was a gambler. His ultimate vice. I have come to his rescue more times than I can count."

"Has he ever been threatened?" I asked.

"There have been times, yes, where, through careless actions, he needed to be dragged back across the moral line."

"Is there any indication he was involved in any high-stakes operations?" Holmes pushed.

"No, nothing that I knew of, but his crowd is fierce. All it would take was for one wrong person to get upset, and they'd bash his head in," said Professor Lovett with eyes burning bright.

"Can you tell us the names of anyone with whom your brother associated in this capacity?"

"Unfortunately not! There may be someone at the University who could tell you. I keep my distance as much as I can."

"Thank you," said Holmes as he stood. Professor Lovett and I followed. "I will see your nephew now. Please send him in."

Professor Lovett nodded and walked out of the door.

"Boy, they want to see you now."

A moment later, Randall entered the room. In his hand, he held a black cane with a silver curved handle. His expression was troubled as he nervously sat before us.

"Hello," he said, looking at each of us in turn.

"Good day, Randall, though I must say that cane there, you have not removed any evidence from the scene?" I asked, as the cane he held was identical to that which lay across his father's body.

"No, Watson, if you observed, his father's cane was heavily worn at the bottom. This stick is clean and looks rarely used," corrected Holmes.

"That is remarkable, Mr Holmes, and true," said Randall. "My father and I both had identical canes made some years back. I've had it with me since the day it was made, but gentlemen, how may I help you? I am most distraught over the death of my father. We were very close, and his loss is most tragic!"

"If you could please recount the events that transpired the day before your father was found, that would be an adequate start," I said, as Holmes leaned back in his chair, tapping his pointer fingers together.

"Yes, let me see. I woke that day rather late, eight-thirty it was. I called for Oswald and had a bath prepared for me. Following my morning meal, I went for a stroll. I walked along the ridges some time, enjoying the breezy air coming in off the ocean. Beyond that, I stopped at the farmers' market to pick up some fruit and returned home. This must have been around one o'clock. I spent the remaining hours of the afternoon in my study. I heard little from the other members of the house, besides Oswald, who came and went with drinks and various other things, and therefore did not see my uncle or father until we had supper together," finished Randall.

"How was your father at supper?" Holmes asked.

"He was in good spirits. Telling us of all the remarkable tasks he's undertaken since his change in role at the university. He seemed very pleased, almost as if nothing on earth could bring him down."

"What of your uncle and father?"

"Yes, well, like all brothers, they can be at each other's necks from time to time. I am sure you are aware that their being here was to 'mend', as it were, their relationship. I trust that if it was not for my own mother's passing away, for she died in childbirth, I believe my father and uncle would have parted many years ago," said Randall. "My uncle is a good man, though very hot-tempered, and not too personable with some people, but he has always been good to me."

"He was not sociable with the locals, I understand," Holmes remarked.

"No, not at all, I preserve the family name in these parts while my father and uncle live and work away. My uncle has never enjoyed mingling with anyone while here. He relishes his privacy and spends hours in the boat."

"Tell us more of your father," said Holmes.

"My father was always very different from my uncle. He enjoyed speaking with new folks and liked hosting parties on the estate when he was here. He was always extremely eccentric. Wherever he was, the people flocked to him. He was, indeed, no stranger, rather everyone's friend."

"You say there was nothing out of the ordinary in your father whatsoever last night?" I asked.

"No, should there have been? What did my uncle say?" asked Randall.

"What can you tell us of your father's gambling habits?" Holmes pressed, ignoring the question.

"He was a gambler, that's true. It wasn't unlike him to lose a decent amount of money one day and then recoup it the next. I know this habit put a fair amount of strain on the relationship between my uncle and father. My uncle always said this habit would find him with his head bashed in one day."

I perked up at Randall's expression, but Holmes remained calm throughout and showed no signs of excitement.

"Hm," uttered Holmes. "Tell me. Could you lead us in the direction of the person, or persons, with whom your father associated in his gambling addiction?"

"Sadly, no, he kept that very private. The only effect we ever had from his gambling were the benefits of the money or the hard times when it was scarce," said he.

"Where did he go to indulge his habit?" I asked.

"I am in the dark on this also, I'm afraid," said Randall with a blank expression.

"Very well, I think we have enough for now. Tell Mr Oswald to wait, we'll call him in," said Holmes.

"Thank you, Mr Holmes. If there is anything I can do for you, please let me know," said young Randall with a nod as he left us, closing the door behind him.

"Fascinating, is it not?" said Holmes as Randall went through the door. "I find it interesting that the two men can say nothing more of the man's gambling addiction other than that he had one."

"Indeed, it seemed they cared little to help him battle this consuming condition," said I. "But tell me, Holmes, what do you think of his brother, Ralph?"

"Yes, he is intriguing. Clearly, he and his brother were very much estranged, and any attempt to heal their relationship had surely failed. There is no sign in any capacity that Professor Lovett was in a forgiving mood," admitted Holmes.

"Then, you suspect him?" I asked.

"The time is not yet ripe to reveal that. Though there is a clue that is striking."

"Which is?" I pressed.

"The victim's wound, Watson. It was in the front. There were no signs of a struggle in the room, nor was there any indication of bruises from a fight."

"Be clear, man."

Holmes sighed. "Professor Lovett indicated that the murderer must have been someone his brother was familiar with, as he was attacked within the manor. There appear to be two possible avenues at this time, and both revolve around this one thing. Whoever attacked Ronald Lovett was indeed no stranger. He knew his attacker. We know now that he kept his gambling life private from his brother and son, so it is possible that someone attacked him as some form of retribution. Money seems to have been no matter, in the end, or a more serious threat could have been made upon the man's family. No, Watson, there is no blackmail, no greed. Just cold-blooded murder," finished Holmes.

"By Jove. Why, yes, I see that now," said I.

"Nevertheless, we are still very far from the finale, Watson. Let us finish our last interview. Bring in Mr Oswald."

As he entered, he kept dabbing his forehead with a cloth, catching beads of sweat that were forming, as he took a seat.

"Hello," he said.

"Good afternoon, would you please recount the events of yesterday for us?" Holmes asked.

"I don't need to. I know who killed dear Master Ronald," said he. His voice was shaky and his perspiration increased.

"My good man, please calm yourself. Are you certain you know who killed Ronald Lovett?" Holmes asked.

"I am," he replied.

"Then, please continue," said Holmes.

"It was his brother, Master Ralph!"

"And you saw this happen?" I asked.

"Well, no, but I heard it," he replied.

"You heard it? Recall the events for us, leaving no detail unsaid!" Holmes urged.

"It was after supper, I remember. Master Ralph had had plenty to drink that night, and I recall him being very squirmy at the table. He never seemed to enjoy having meals with the family. He'd always drown himself in wine."

"So he was drunk?" I clarified.

"Oh yes, very much so," replied Mr Oswald. "He got very angry at the table when his brother was speaking about his job. I know the resentment runs deep and Master Ralph has never forgiven his brother for snatching the role of principal from under him, but as I always say, you must fight for what you want at all costs."

"Even if that cost ruins your family?" Holmes asked. Mr Oswald continued, ignoring Holmes's question.

"Well, like I said, Master Ralph was very angry that night, and he stormed out of the dining hall. I cleared up after him, and the late Master Ronald said he was going out for a smoke in the garden house. He asked me to bring him a pot of tea after I was done. So I did just that. When I approached, I heard raised voices. It was Master Ralph and Ronald. They were bickering horribly with each other. I heard a loud bang, like a fist hitting the wall. I got closer because I wanted to listen, and I heard Master Ralph say, 'You always gloat about stealing everything from me!' Master Ronald replied, 'Isn't the big brother meant to be the bully and always get his way? It's not my issue that you are not alpha enough to put me in my place, and I am forced to make our family name stronger than you ever could!'

"Then, Master Ralph shouted something like, 'You are a swine! You take and take with no care for anyone! Just like you took my wife and ruined her! Just like you ruined your poor boy's mother! And just like you've ruined me! And after all the times I bailed you out, paid your debts. You are an ungrateful git, and someone will teach you a lesson one day!' Master Ralph gave a cry and finished saying, 'Get that bloody cane out of my face before I bash it into your skull!'

"I heard footsteps, and the door swung open, and Master Ralph walked out into the night. He paused and looked back; I'd never seen him so angry before. For a moment, I worried that he spotted me, but he carried on. I knocked on the door and brought the tea tray in for Master Ronald. He didn't respond to me whatsoever and just sat in a chair holding his old cane. I excused myself, and when I stepped back into the house, I passed Master Ralph, who was still brewing and staring out the door at the glass structure. The next morning, I knocked on Master Ronald's door, as I usually woke him at seven o'clock. I noticed Master Ralph was out, and Master Randall was yet to wake. I received no response from Mr Ronald, so I opened the door and found his bed and night clothes untouched.

"I looked through the house but saw no one. So I decided to check the garden house. It was out there that I saw the body of Master Ronald with his head horribly beaten. I ran inside the house and Master Ralph was coming in the front door, saying he was out for a morning walk. I feared telling him what I knew about last night and just told him that something horrible had happened to his brother. That's when I left the house to send a wire for local authorities. I told a few folks along the way, simply for my own protection, in case something happened to me. Then, not long after, I returned, and you two showed up," finished Mr Oswald.

"An incriminating story, to say the least, and does not put Professor Lovett in a good place," said I.

We then heard muffled angry voices outside. We raced out of the study, and found Professor Lovett and his nephew arguing in the kitchen.

"Where is it!?" shouted young Randall.

"I don't know! I never knew where it was!" Professor Lovett replied.

"What's the issue?" Holmes asked.

"We've got a problem, Mr Holmes. Something very precious is missing," said Randall.

"What is it?" I asked.

"My brother was the holder of a very precious stone. It was a rare red ruby that he found on an expedition in Africa. He held it in a safe somewhere on the grounds. That is the most I knew of its whereabouts. My nephew knew the location of the safe; he decided to check it while you were speaking with Oswald, and is accusing me of its disappearance," said Professor Lovett.

"It wasn't Oswald!" said Randall. We were then interrupted by a knock on the main door.

"That must be the authorities!" cried Mr Oswald. We four stood while he answered the door. Sure enough, there stood one officer and one inspector. "Thank you for coming!" said Mr Oswald.

"No trouble, I am Inspector Jones. This is Officer Hayter. Tell us what has happened," said he.

"I believe I can be of help. I am Mr Sherlock Holmes, of London…"

"Yes, we know who you are, Mr Holmes. But we are more than capable of handling this affair ourselves," Inspector Jones acknowledged with little care.

"Then you shall follow your path and I shall follow mine," said Holmes.

"I should think not, Mr Holmes. You can follow my path, as it will be the only one I will allow you to follow. They might love you in London, and you might get all the attention you want from the foreign press, but you will not receive special treatment from me. You work with me, or you don't work at all," barked Inspector Jones.

"Very well, if you would like it that way, we shall work with you. Consult me as you wish. I will kindly tell you all I know and where I got up to in my investigation," said Holmes.

"Our investigation," the Inspector corrected.

"Yes, of course. Our investigation."

We were taken back to the body, and Inspector Jones wandered around. Holmes and I stood back and watched him work. "Tell me, now, what you have learnt, Mr Holmes?" he asked.

"We know that Ronald Lovett was a gambler and, on occasion, got into trouble due to his addiction. We also know that he and his brother were not on the best of terms," said Holmes.

"Aha! And looks like we have a boot print in the blood!" said Inspector Jones.

"Pardon?" asked Holmes.

"Yes, right there. We can use this to check the shoes worn by the members of the household, especially if you say his brother and he had bad blood," said Inspector Jones.

"I must say, I inspected this room earlier, and there was, in fact, no boot print," said Holmes.

"Well, clearly you missed something, Mr Holmes," said he. "Officer Hayter, please inspect the grounds while I speak with the household members." Inspector Jones took a measurement of the print, and he stormed back into the house. "Professor, might I have your boot, please?" he said as the Professor awkwardly took off his boot. He handed it to the Inspector, who checked his measurements. "I need to see your room, please."

"What's the problem?" Professor Lovett asked.

"Please, just show me," Inspector Jones insisted. We followed the two men up the stairs and into Professor Lovett's private room. Immediately, the Inspector began sorting through the pairs of shoes in the closet. He leaned back and sighed.

"What's the problem?" Holmes asked.

"None of these are the shoe," he said.

"I fear you are jumping in too fast, Inspector," said Holmes.

"Mr Holmes, please, I do not need your advice. Within minutes of my arrival, I found a vital clue; one that you missed. You London boys think you can catch it all. You have no respect for anyone."

"Holmes," said I, "why not just leave this. You don't deserve this treatment."

"No, Watson, we will ride this out."

*****

Inspector Jones proceeded to question each household member himself. However, he did not allow Holmes or me to sit inside, so we waited in the hall. "This really is most degrading, Holmes!" I said. "Why are you letting this Inspector do this?"

"Because he found a boot print," Holmes explained.

"What do you mean?"

"You were with me while I searched that entire room. There was no boot print. I would have seen it." I admit that I was too overcome with annoyance to clearly see what Holmes had, and the finding of this boot print was deeply troubling him.

"So, where did it come from?" I asked.

"Exactly, Watson! Where did it come from? Who put it there, and why?" We then heard someone coming inside. It was Officer Hayter. He rushed in on Inspector Jones and asked to speak at once.

"Inspector, I have something," he said. Inspector Jones quickly got up and met him in the hallway, shutting the study door. I was not sure whether Inspector Jones was fully aware of our presence as he continued to speak with Officer Hayter, paying no attention to Holmes and me as we stood and listened.

"This better be good for pulling me out of there!" said he.

"It is. I found these," said Officer Hayter, opening up a tin container and pulling out a ruffled shirt and a pair of black boots. Both were covered in blood. "These are the same size as Professor Lovett," he said. "But I also found this," he pulled out a slip of paper. "It was in the Professor's room, inside a hollowed-out book."

The paper was a map of the garden house that showed the location where the ruby was hidden, including the safe's combination.

"All right, give those to me," said Inspector Jones, taking the container into his hands and putting the apparel back inside. Inspector Jones stepped back into the room, leaving the door open. He sat once more with Professor Lovett, setting the tin container on the floor. "Your shoes, Professor. They are made by Smiths & Co. in Oxford, is that correct?"

"That is yes."

"How many pairs of shoes do you own?"

"I have five. But some are very old."

"Yet, when I looked in your room, I saw only four."

"Then you must have miscounted."

"Or perhaps, you tried to hide a certain incriminating pair?"

"For heaven's sake, what are you saying, Inspector?!" The Inspector walked around the room with his hands shoved deep in his pockets. "We also have this," and he pulled out the map. Professor Lovett stood in shock.

"Where did you find this!?" he shouted.

"Calm down. You know very well it was you. You killed your brother. He messed up your life, ruined your career, and you finally snapped. You took his cane, and you beat his head in, and you took his precious stone. Where have you hidden it?"

"This is outrageous! I have no clue what you mean!"

"Unfortunately for you, Mr Oswald witnessed your fight after supper, and there were some strong words being tossed around. Now, oh now, it's clear. We have these," said Inspector Jones, reaching into the tin container and pulling out the shoes and slamming them down on the table.

"Those are my shoes!" roared Professor Lovett.

"Yes, I'm sure it's a surprise to see them. You thought you hid them well. And you must have thought you were going to get clean away. I mean, not even the great Sherlock Holmes was able to find these! But here they are with one of your shirts, covered in your own brother's blood!"

"I didn't do it. I didn't kill my brother!"

"Stay calm. I must put you under arrest for the murder of Ronald Lovett. A judge can decide your fate," said Inspector Jones. He turned the Professor around and bound his hands. Mr Oswald and Randall Lovett rushed in.

"What's happened?" Oswald asked.

"Inspector Jones found the killer," said I.

"Uncle! Uncle, why?" yelled Randall.

"Boy, it wasn't me, I promise you!" said Professor Lovett.

"Professor, I must insist you keep your mouth shut for now," said Inspector Jones.

"Holmes, Mr Holmes, please…" said Professor Lovett, who went silent when Inspector Jones punched him in the stomach. He passed the Professor over to Officer Hayter, who carted him away.

"Well, well, well. Looks like your services were not required here, Mr Holmes. Your reputation certainly didn't hold its weight," said Inspector Jones with a smug look upon his face.

"Holmes has done far more for society than you ever will!" I roared.

"Calm yourself, Watson. I can fight my own battles. I only choose to fight battles that are worth it," said Holmes.

"Looks like you are a poor loser, Mr Holmes. Well, if you don't mind, I must ask you to leave the property now. We are no longer in need of your services."

"Very well," said Holmes, turning to me with a nod, and we left the estate.

*****

The sun was setting, and Holmes and I were sitting on two large rocks watching the tide roll back in. He was silent, tossing a few rocks into the water from time to time. "By Jove, did you see that?" Holmes perked up.

"See what?" I asked. Then, I looked out into the ocean and saw fins and puffs of water exploding from the waves. "What is it?" I asked.

"Looks like dolphins, Watson. This is indeed a rare treat," said Holmes, watching the large water beasts swim around.

When the animals had gone, we made our way up the beach, and I offered to fetch ourselves a pint at the inn before we retired back to our cottage. We took a seat at a corner table, and the same woman who served us before brought us our drinks.

"How're you two? Had a good day?" she asked.

"Eventful, ma'am," said Holmes.

"You must be thinkin' this place is rough, what with all the drama goin' on. A murder. My Lord, things like this never happen around here. Sure, the odd sailor will fall overboard, but nothing like this. And to think, that nice ole Professor done gone and did the whole thing."

"I'm sorry, how do you know this already?" I asked.

"Oh, the ole butler, Oswald, he's good friends with us. He tells us all the gossip. Like just the other day, he said that it was bad business with Mr Randall Lovett and his fiancée, Miss Rebeka Stonewall. Then, the next day, they end their engagement. Still don't know the whole details. Mr Randall's been quiet about it and has not shown any sympathy or sorrow in being done with it, but I heard she was sleeping with another man. I can't judge, though, I just got rumours. That ole Oswald's full of them," said the lady, still holding the tray with our drinks on it. "Oh my, forgive me. Here are your drinks. I'll let you be," she said, putting them on the table.

"She is quite the character. These local folk would hardly be able to survive a day in our line of work, wouldn't you say, Holmes?"

"Watson, this case is not over. There is a game afoot. Inspector Jones is simply being ignorant. If you would excuse me, Watson, I would like to be alone with my

119

thoughts. I shall meet you at the cottage," said Holmes. He took one gulp of his pint and dashed out the door.

*****

After finishing my drink, with the sun fully set, I walked by the moonlight, which was particularly bright, down to the end of the small dock to watch the night waves and enjoy its calming effect. I sat down and let my legs hang off; after some time, I lay down to look up at the clear, black sky, dazzling with stars. I must have lain there for nearly an hour before I felt the need to return to our cottage. I took the path back up the steep stone stairs and walked along the cliffside path. I had a small torch with me, which helped to guide my way. As I approached the vine-encased tunnel, I heard a pair of voices at the other end, where a small cottage was dimly lit.

"I'm sorry, I want nothing to do with you!" said the voice of a young woman.

"But please! It's all over, nothing is standing in our way anymore!" said a man whose voice sounded very familiar to me.

"What do you mean? It's all over?" asked the young woman.

"You know exactly what I mean!" replied the man.

"I don't want to have anything to do with you or your family! Not anymore! No, I must ask you to leave," the young woman stated in a firm voice.

"Then, tell me, where is it? I know you have it! I won't leave until you give it back!" the man cried. I could see his shadowy figure reach out towards the woman. I decided to make my presence clear to these two. I continued to walk through the tunnel, making a bit more noise to get their attention.

"Who is there?" echoed the man's voice. "Name yourself!"

"John Watson," said I. The figure, in a sudden twist, let go of the woman and ran off into the night. I approached the woman whom I could see, under the moonlight, who was frightened. "Are you all right, Miss?" I asked.

"Yes, I am fine. Just shaken a tiny bit," she said.

"What's your name?" I asked.

"Rebeka Stonewall," she said.

"Forgive my forwardness, but are you the Miss Stonewall who recently had an engagement ended?"

"Yes, I am she."

"Was that Randall Lovett just now?" I pressed further.

"It was. He's absolutely terrifying right now! I know there is a horrible business with his father, Ronald, and his uncle was arrested for the murder, but sometimes I think I need protection from him," she admitted.

"What was he so eager to retrieve from you?" I asked.

"He wants the engagement ring back. But I don't have it. My family took it, but he doesn't believe me," she said.

"I am here with Mr Sherlock Holmes; he's a formidable detective, from London. If you have any concerns regarding the Lovetts, please come to see us tomorrow. Holmes has been looking into the case, and he might find your information useful," said I.

"The Sherlock Holmes? Of 221b Baker Street?" she asked.

"The very one," said I.

"Oh, I would be very grateful for your help! I will come to see you tomorrow morning when I've had a chance to calm my nerves."

"Very well. Find us at Glan-y-mor Cottage." Miss Stonewall thanked me and walked back into the small cottage. I continued back to our cottage, where I found myself alone. I left a note for Holmes informing him of Miss Stonewall's arrival and retired for the night.

When I woke, I found Holmes downstairs holding the note that I had left. "Good morning, Watson, what is this?" he asked.

"A most peculiar incident, Holmes," said I. "On my journey home, I came across young Randall Lovett and Miss Stonewall, who were having a heated argument outside her cottage regarding her engagement ring. She says Randall worries her, so I informed her that if she needed any aid, to contact us, which she said she would do today."

"Good man, Watson. Her perspective would prove useful, I'm sure."

"Where did you go last night?" I asked.

"Watson, whilst I conducted my investigation, who was about the house?" he asked, disregarding my question.

"What do you mean? You know who was there," said I.

"Yes, but did you see them at all times?"

"I suppose not, apart from Professor Lovett."

"Exactly! Apart from Professor Lovett. While we questioned the Professor, someone was at the same time framing him!"

"Frame? Are you so sure?"

"It's all too convenient, Watson."

"The only people out of sight were Mr Oswald and Randall. What cause do they have to kill Ronald?" I asked.

"Time will tell. Though I cannot stand by when I know that there was no boot print in the blood or a tin container containing the boots and shirt. Someone is framing Professor Lovett, but to what purpose? Professor Lovett's anger towards his brother was no secret, nor was his short-fused temper. The motive is clearly there, but he didn't do it.

There is a double threat being played. Not only is Professor Lovett suddenly the murderer, but, furthermore, even my own skills in deduction are suddenly and seriously degraded. Though, as it were, the story fits. The professor who hates his brother suddenly snaps and kills his brother, then steals his precious stone in revenge. But one thing remains. If that were the case, why would Professor Lovett still be there the next day? He clearly had no plan of leaving, because he did not commit the murder."

"Remarkable!" said I. "So you believe it to be Mr Oswald or Randall?"

"I do not want to jump to a conclusion. Not until I have all the facts," said Holmes. There was a knock on our door. I opened it and found Inspector Jones standing there.

"May I speak with Mr Holmes?" he asked.

"Please, come in," said I.

"What can I do for you?" Holmes asked.

"The night has been long, and I am tangled in a web that I cannot free myself from. There has been another murder," said the Inspector.

"Another murder! Who?" I asked.

"Miss Rebeka Stonewall," said the Inspector.

"Randall's ex-fiancée," said Holmes, and Inspector Jones nodded.

"She was killed in the exact same way as Ronald Lovett. Her head was beaten severely. She was found by the housemaid, who had no information of any great use," said Inspector Jones.

"If you are ready to listen to me, then I will help you!" said Holmes.

"If that is the extent of the scolding, I am grateful. I deserve more after my actions, but yes, I do need your help, Mr Holmes," said he.

"Then I shall help you. I shall need to see the woman's body right away."

*****

We spent a few moments preparing, then left the cottage. I found it hard to believe that this poor woman was suddenly and tragically killed. I felt that I should not have left her so soon last night. Not after what I had witnessed. Entering her cottage, we found the body lying on the floor of her room. "This could not have been long after I saw her, Holmes," said I. "She's wearing the same clothing, and the blood has had ample time to dry."

"You saw her last night?" Inspector Jones asked.

"I did on my way home. She was having an argument with young Randall Lovett over her engagement ring. He acted aggressively, and when I made my presence known, he ordered me to identify myself. He then ran off when I announced my name."

"This is disturbing. Do none of these Lovetts have any kind of moral compass?" the Inspector asked. "We'll need to bring him in for questioning at once. The only thing we found on her body," continued Inspector Jones, "was this," and he handed Holmes a photograph. Holmes took it and put his glass to it. It was an image of Ronald Lovett and Randall.

"What do you see, Watson?" said Holmes.

"I see Mr Ronald Lovett standing on the steps next to Randall. It appears to be at a university. The image looks recent, and they are holding their black canes," said I.

"Odd, is it not?" said Holmes.

"I can hardly see how. The poor girl has had her heart broken, her engagement called off, and her ex-fiancée beating at her door at late hours demanding items back. I can imagine she was simply remembering better times when she was attacked," said I.

"But it is suggestive." Holmes then looked at the body. Her face was crushed beyond recognition. "Why did she die?" Holmes asked. He ran his glass over her from top to bottom. He jumped up and looked right at me. "Watson, was there anything strange about your incident last night? Did she say anything to you other than her fears over Randall? Give me her words exactly," Holmes demanded. As I recalled the conversation, I remembered a singular moment that I thought was rather odd.

"I recall that she referred to Randall's father as Ronald. I found it to be rather informal." Holmes paced the room, mumbling to himself. He sat on the woman's bed. He then knelt back down and looked at the woman's hands, making grunts as he examined her fingers. Holmes began running his hands along the wooden floorboards. "What are you doing?" I pressed. Holmes, with his head underneath the woman's bed, made another groan. There was a snapping noise, and he discarded a plank of wood. Moments later, he rose to his feet, holding a cloth in his hand. Unfolding it, he revealed a giant red ruby.

"I think we found the real reason Randall was in such a state last night," said Holmes. I reached out and picked up the ruby.

"How did you know where to find that!?" asked Inspector Jones. Holmes then lifted his hand, showing a feather.

"Her fingernails are broken, and there are splinters under her nails. She was recently scratching at something. That board under her bed has marks that correspond with her nails. Clearly something was hidden beneath," said Holmes. "Something else is clear. I think you need to rethink the position of Professor Lovett, wouldn't you say, Inspector?" The Inspector's face turned white.

"So she took the ruby! But how? When did she get it?" the Inspector returned.

"That is what we must find out, and I feel in doing so all the loose threads will tie together!" said Holmes. "Now, something we can safely assume is that she was hiding this ruby from whoever came in and killed her. That means that the killer didn't get what they wanted. The Lovetts and Miss Stonewall have most certainly tangled themselves up in a dire mess, and this photograph is a very telling piece of evidence."

"The photograph? How so?" Inspector Jones asked.

"In good time, let us be off at once to the Lovett estate! After Watson's encounter last night, they are the obvious suspects to see."

"Agreed! What shall we do with the ruby?" Inspector Jones asked.

"I shall hold it for the moment," said Holmes. "Now, we have no time to lose!" We quickly jumped into the Inspector's cart and were trudging along down the dirt path towards the main road. Soon, we approached the Lovett estate. Mr Oswald answered the door upon our call. "Hello, gentlemen. How may I help you?" he asked.

"May we see Randall?" Inspector Jones countered.

"Unfortunately, he is out. He's gone down to the markets for a bit of fresh air, and left just moments ago."

"Then, would you mind if Doctor Watson and Officer Hayter remain while we go find him in the village? It's important that we speak with him. It's regarding his uncle and the missing ruby," said Holmes. Mr Oswald looked disturbed by this news.

"Yes, of course… Please come in… I will make you a drink while you wait," he stammered.

"We shall be back with you soon, Watson," said Holmes, and he and Inspector Jones left.

*****

Officer Hayter and I sat in the dining hall. Oswald brought in tea. "Please, have a nice drink. Would you care for food, my good men? There are fresh scones, not even an hour old."

"That would be excellent, thank you," said Officer Hayter.

I put Holmes's techniques into practice. I recalled that, while I sat with Professor Lovett, Oswald refused to sit with us while Holmes searched the house. Officer Hayter poured sugar into his tea and began to stir it. The more my mind raced over the events, the more Mr Oswald became suspicious to me. He had gone in and out several times while Professor Lovett and I sat in the dining hall. He had the perfect cover. Officer Hayter put his tea to his lips and sipped it.

"Would you care for a cup, Doctor Watson?" he asked.

"No, thank you," I replied. "Don't you find it odd? Fresh scones, only an hour old, yet there is no aroma in the air to indicate anyone has been cooking."

Suddenly, Officer Hayter began to choke. I dipped my finger in the tea and let a drop fall on my tongue. I spat it out on the floor. Poisoned!

I didn't have much time. I dashed into the kitchen and tore through the cabinets until I found a container of salt. I rushed back and poured it into the officer's mouth. He struggled but swallowed it and, a moment later, was violently sick as he forced the poison out of his body. I sat with him for what felt like hours, but was nothing more than a few minutes. He began to breathe normally again, and his heart rate slowed to a more stable pace. I moved him into another room and sat him down.

"You will be fine. Stay here. I'm off to find Oswald!" said I, my heart racing.

Revolver in hand, I raced through the house, trying to find the butler. He had had ample time to escape while I had treated Officer Hayter, but he anticipated that I would drink as well. It was possible that he was hiding until we were dead, then he would do away with us, tell Holmes and Inspector Jones we had left, and give himself a chance to flee.

I turned a corner and, suddenly, saw pieces of stone fly into the air as an iron rod swung at me, nearly striking me in the face and shattering the corner of the wall. I fell back, landing on my shoulder. My old army injury began to ache as I came down hard upon it. My gun fell from my hands, and I tried quickly to pull myself together. Mr Oswald stood before me, holding the iron rod. He dragged it across the floor as he approached.

"So it was you. You killed them! You framed Professor Lovett—why? For the missing ruby?" I asked.

"Me? No. I've never killed anyone in my life—until now. But I would do anything for the boy, Master Randall," said Mr Oswald.

"Randall?" I asked.

He raised the iron rod into the air and charged at me. As he did, there was a loud bang, and he lost his footing, falling over. I turned to see Officer Hayter leaning on a doorframe on the other side of the room. His face was pale, and he was shaking. I picked myself up and ran over to him.

"Thank you, my man. You saved my life!" I exclaimed.

"Just like you did for me. Thank you, Doctor," he sighed.

I took his arm, and we approached Mr Oswald, who was lying on the floor. Hayter had shot him in the leg, and Mr Oswald was clutching the wound in pain.

However, the adrenaline was too much for the old man, and he passed out. We cuffed his hands and left him on the floor as we waited for Holmes and Inspector Jones to return. I had taken Officer Hayter into the kitchen to tend to him a little more when we heard the front door swing open.

"Oswald! Holmes and that damned Inspector are looking for me. Did you tell them I was in the village? You are a fool. I am running out of time, and I cannot be dealing with pointless issues such as these!" cried the voice of Randall through the house. "Oswald!" He saw his butler on the floor. "What's happened? Are you here? You fiends! Show yourselves. I told you I would get it—I had until tonight! If you killed him, I will kill you!" he roared.

I motioned to Officer Hayter to be quiet, and we slowly made our way to the back door. I hid Officer Hayter in the bushes and carefully approached the house again. I could still hear Mr Randall shouting from within. He burst through the back door and raged towards the garden house. He screamed when he entered. I slowly approached, positioned myself against the brick siding, and peered in through the window.

"How are you alive? I... I... You should be dead!" he yelled.

"But I'm not, am I?" said the voice of a young woman—a familiar voice.

"I killed you! Last night, I killed you!"

"Fortunately for me, you did not. What you did do is kill my double," she said. Peering in, I realised I was looking at Miss Stonewall. "Don't worry," she continued, "I've placed plenty of evidence that will lead them straight back to you."

"A double? Don't try to fool me with these tricks!"

"She's been with me the whole time! We were masters of disguise, you little man. Take a guess as to who the maid was who 'found' me dead. It was I. I let the police question me over my own murder."

"You are a poisonous Jezebel! You made me kill the wrong person," he said.

"I am more of a Delilah. I found your weakness, and I tore you apart. Greed—money—it's the root of all evil. And the loss of my 'double' was necessary for this greater purpose," she said.

"Give me the ruby back now! Let me pay off the debt! We can settle our scores another way!" said he.

"Do you have any idea who you are paying off?" she asked. "I have the stone which was the payment, yet it doesn't matter. The order was given to kill you upon payment. But you see, I need a way out myself. Now they will think you killed me for the decoy stone I left behind.

They will find you dead. I will walk away a free woman and use the real ruby to begin a new life, far, far away. It was rather convenient that Mr Holmes showed up as well. Even he cannot see through this blind spot and will only help to solidify my escape and your demise. I think I've planned a better end for you—certainly a kinder demise than they could give you. Think about the poetic justice: the woman you murder is actually the woman who murders you!"

I was then startled when Holmes placed his hand on my shoulder. He indicated that I should be quiet, and I nodded. He leaned in close to me.

"We followed him here. I'm glad to see you are safe."

"Holmes, she has the ruby! Randall killed his father and framed his uncle," I whispered.

"Yes, I know. The ruby in the house was a fake. I noticed it when Inspector Jones and I left," said Holmes.

"There's going to be a gunfight soon. We need to stop this," said I.

"Very well. Inspector Jones is going around the back. We can surprise them from the front," said Holmes. The two of us stood up, and Holmes walked into the garden house. "Unfortunately, my dear Miss Stonewall and Mr Randall Lovett," Holmes interrupted, "I now know that the ruby in the cottage was a fake—placed there as a decoy to frame."

"Holmes, you swine!" roared Randall at our sudden entrance. Miss Stonewall kept her face firm.

"It took me a while to notice the ruby was a decoy, but I am a little rusty in my observation of rare stones. Furthermore, neither of you can get away. I know the facts, and I have passed them on. Which means, Miss Stonewall, your plan of escape is flawed. Whomever you work for, they will know of your failure and find you."

"Mr Holmes, you have greatly inconvenienced me," said Miss Stonewall. With no warning, she fired her gun, hitting Mr Randall in the chest. Holmes raced to the man, but he was dead. She ran, and we chased after her through a back door. Another shot was fired, and Inspector Jones lay on the ground holding his arm. I stopped, but he urged me to follow Holmes. The woman ran, turning from time to time to fire a shot at us. She suddenly stopped, and we realised there was nowhere for her to go. She stood on a cliff, and below her the raging ocean crashed against the sharp rocks.

"The game is up, Miss Stonewall. You cannot escape," said Holmes.

"There is nowhere I can go, Mr Holmes. If they know I'm alive, they will find me."

"Who are they?" I asked.

"Don't you know?" she said with a devilish grin.

"Enlighten us," said Holmes.

"We are everywhere, Mr Holmes. I have spent the last two years waiting for this moment—my freedom."

"A freedom that was schemed out of the habitual gambling habits of the Lovetts," clarified Holmes.

"Randall was just like his father—a gambler. I was put in place to ruin him and claim his fortune—the entire fortune. The job itself was easy, as both men were fools, especially for me.

"It was an easy way of robbing him legally, you see. My employer was more than happy with the arrangement. As Randall's addiction grew stronger and his bank emptied, I was told to use the same tactic on the father, so I urged Randall to get money from his father if he wanted to continue. We drained the son, and we would drain the father through the son."

"So what changed in the plan?" I asked.

"I suspect things went awry when Randall caught his father with Miss Stonewall. You were having an affair, correct?" pressed Holmes.

"You are clever, Mr Holmes," she began.

"Wasn't difficult. Not many fiancées will call their soon-to-be father-in-law by his first name, nor will they have a picture of them, as you did," said Holmes.

"I was seeing Ronald in secret, and Randall caught us. He was so cold and fierce about it. He said nothing, just broke off our engagement, and he refused to speak to me," she said.

"So he killed his father because he caught you two together, figured he could frame his uncle and potentially win you back with his new fortune," said Holmes.

"Rather perfect, isn't it? His uncle hated his brother so much. Take his father out of the way, frame the uncle for murder—he'd surely hang for it. Then steal the ruby, pay the debts, and inherit his father's and uncle's money, which we would be able to continually drain," said Miss Stonewall.

"But you got the ruby first, for your own reasons, which threw off his plan. That sent him into a frenzy; he'd suspect that you had it due to your affair, and he'd come after you— probably kill you if he could. So you worked it out in advance to frame him for your death, kill him, and stage it as a suicide, which would be easily believable, and you'd vanish," concluded Holmes.

"Exactly! Everything fell into place so perfectly, especially when the Inspector hated you so passionately," said Miss Stonewall.

"Sadly, though, you were overzealous. Had you simply left Randall alone, you could have escaped, and he would have been charged with his father's murder due to a clue you left at the scene of your supposed murder. The photograph —it shows the two holding their canes. The cane found on Ronald's body was scratched and in poor condition, yet the one in the picture was smooth and clean, while Randall's was scratched. He clearly swapped canes with his father in some manner of deluded victory," said Holmes. "Now, I'm sorry, but you must come with me."

"I'm afraid I cannot do that. I must be free of them," she said. "There is no way out, except one, now." And she fell backwards off the cliff.

We raced to the edge and saw her body broken on the rocks below. Lying just above her head was the real ruby. It sparkled beautifully in the sunlight, creating an odd contrast to that terrible scene. The waters below were rough, and as we looked down upon Miss Stonewall's broken body, a large wave crashed over the rocks and swept the body and the stone out to sea.

*****

We returned and aided Inspector Jones and Officer Hayter, who both required medical attention. Inspector Jones had a surface wound and was only in need of a few stitches. Officer Hayter took a little more time to mend. Holmes and I informed Inspector Jones of what had happened with Miss Stonewall, and a boat was sent out to search for her body, though it was never found.

Holmes and I remained in Morfa Nefyn for the remainder of our attempted holiday, though the latter half was indeed much quieter than the former. Professor Lovett was released and returned home, while the butler, Mr

Oswald, was sent to prison for his role in the affair. Professor Lovett contacted us and wished to have an audience. We dined with him, and he thanked us for our service, but beyond that, we did not see him again for the rest of our trip. On the day of our departure, Inspector Jones made a special journey to see Holmes and me off, which did bring Holmes a measure of cheer.

*****

When we returned to Baker Street, the rains had gone, and the sun was shining brightly.

"It's good to be back, eh, Watson?" said Holmes.

"Indeed it is," said I.

"Mr Holmes," said Mrs Hudson. "This came for you just now." Holmes took the letter and read it. His face fell into deep concern.

"Are you all right, Holmes?" I asked. With a distressed look upon his face, he handed me the letter, which read:

Mr Holmes,

We cannot be held responsible for what happens to those who continuously interfere with our matters. Though you have been but a small inconvenience, nevertheless, you have caused several troublesome delays in our operations. Take this as a friendly warning. Abandon your investigations, or your body will be shattered upon the rocks.

Peer

"A curious signature," said I.

"There is a strange game afoot. This is clearly a warning that stems from our endeavours in Wales, as it mirrors Miss Stonewall's death."

"Yet 'Peer'—we've seen this before," said I.

"Yes, 'Peer' is undoubtedly the organisation in which Miss Stonewall was so deeply entangled," said Holmes. "Though it is clear we are getting close to uncovering something significant, Watson. This name has appeared many times over the past few months. I daresay there is a grand scheme that is infecting all of Britain. This organisation has left no corner untouched. The fog, Watson —the fog has spread far and wide."

He walked over to his bay window with a cigarette and match in hand. Lighting it, he looked out at the street below.

"I must re-devote my attention to uncovering Peer."

A Study In Clockwork

An Unexpected Parcel at Baker Street

As I reminisce over these cases of my friend Sherlock
Holmes, I realise how tragic and horrifying some of these
events were. I note that on many of these occasions, it put
Holmes and me on the verge of death, from which we
barely escaped. These affairs, however, were singularly
unique and yet so intrinsically linked that I could not share
one without the other. At the same time, the official public
records regarding these cases have been so distorted that
some readers may view this telling as nothing more than
dramatised fiction. Of one thing I can assure the public:
these events are true. I still carry with me the scars from this
affair, and if one uses the great powers of deduction, which
my good friend Mr Sherlock Holmes employs, one will be
able to see the cracks and holes within the official
statements. Though I never fully understood how Holmes
could be at peace with such weak testimonies, which were
mostly void of his assistance, flooding the newsagents. For
Holmes, though, if the puzzle was complete in his mind,
there was nothing more that needed to be done.
Nevertheless, an undeniable fact stands firm; had it not been
for Mr Sherlock Holmes, a reign of terror would have
descended upon England and rapidly spread like an
infectious poison, consuming all Europe and, perhaps, the
globe.

*****

It was on the morning of the eighteenth of May, 1899, when
I sat in the study reading a recent medical journal. Holmes
had been in and out for several weeks, staying up late and

eating next to nothing. I always found his mood somewhat intolerable when he became so engrossed in an investigation. As I sat there and read, he burst into the study with a great shout.

"Watson! After weeks of careful study and in-depth research, I have begun to unravel the mystery! I have pulled the thread that will lead us to the most stunning and yet obvious conclusion." He threw his arms about as he walked around the study.

"Mr Holmes, do try to keep it down, it is rather early for all this shouting," said Mrs Hudson, standing in the door.

"Woman, please, this is no time for interruptions!" Holmes exclaimed.

"Well, I beg your pardon, but there is a package for you at the door," she informed. "When I answered the knock, no one was there, but a large box, too heavy for me to carry, had been left with your name."

"Curious, Watson, come help me fetch it then," said Holmes. Outside the front door was, indeed, a large wooden container. It stood about four feet high and two feet wide. Holmes and I each took a side and began to lift. With great effort, we hefted it from the ground and carried it inside.

"Good Lord, Holmes! What is inside this?" I asked.

"I'm not sure. Once we get it into the study, I'll examine it," he replied.

Picking it up again, we ascended the stairs. There was a trail of damage behind us, as the box slipped from my hands on several occasions, leaving marks on the stairs and walls.

"Don't worry, Mrs Hudson," called Holmes. "All repairs will be taken care of."

I could hear her sigh heavily, looking at what we had done, but she replied with a kind "very well," and left us to our investigation. The box rested in the centre of the study. I sat in my chair, and Holmes, smoking his pipe packed with some of the blackest tobacco he owned, began to walk around the container, circling it like a predator.

"You were not expecting any delivery at all?" I asked.

"None whatsoever, your guess is as good as mine as to the contents resting inside," said Holmes.

"Then open it, shall we?" I asked energetically. Holmes pulled an iron rod from the fireplace and wedged it between the side of the box and the lid. With a swift downward pull and a loud snap, the lid cracked open on one corner. Holmes continued this until three corners were loose.

"Help me now, Watson," Holmes struggled.

I walked over, and we began to lift the lid, popping the fourth nail and releasing the wooden seal. The top came down with a reverberating bang. I half expected Mrs Hudson to rush up and enquire about us. Looking down inside the box, I saw a fair amount of shredded paper and cloth that had been used as a cushion to protect whatever was beneath.

A note rested on top, which we read: Do Not Lift.

"We'll need to collapse the sides then," sighed Holmes.

Both he and I began tugging away at the corners and loosening the nails which held this wooden container together. As one side came down, papers and cloth spilt out onto the floor.

"Whatever it is, they surely did not wish for it to break!" I said.

A short time later, all four sides were flat on the floor, and there, before us, sat an object some three feet tall and a foot and a half wide. The object was covered with ratty cloth and tied with thick string, which Holmes and I began to cut gingerly. As we pulled the covering off, we found a beautifully crafted automaton that sat before a miniature piano.

"What do you make of it, Watson?" asked Holmes.

"It certainly is a wonder," said I. "Why is it here?"

"A question we have no answer for, yet." We both marvelled at the beautifully crafted woman automaton. "The artisan has done remarkable detailing, I say."

Holmes was quite right. The doll's face was painted immaculately. Its lips were perfectly lined with red, and its hair was light brown and styled eloquently. It wore a traditional Englishwoman's gown with a lovely flower design. The doll's piano was polished and reflected as vividly as a mirror. What I found most disturbing about this clockwork doll was its eyes. They were black and hollow, void of a soul.

"How do you suppose it works?" I asked.

"It would wind up in the back; go have a look," ordered Holmes. I walked around the back and saw a slot for a key.

"There's no key!" I reported.

"Interesting," said he.

"Holmes, correct me, but this looks like it's a Pierr Jaquet-Droz original."

"The design is unmistakable. It's clearly based on Pierr Jaquet-Droz's creation, though this is most certainly not an original."

"How can you tell?" I pressed.

"The craftsmanship is superb, and whoever made it imitated the style very carefully," he continued. "However, the first point of difference is in the eyes, which are lifeless. Jaquet-Droz's creations have blue eyes; this one does not. The colour of the skin is, I believe, three shades darker than the original as well; and, as you can see, it has a more realistic tone." He continued examining the doll.

"Well, whoever the real maker is, their work is commendable. Still, why send it to us?" I questioned.

"Halloa, halloa, halloa!" said Holmes. He pulled a black metal object from the doll's hair. "The key!"

"What made you look there?" I asked.

"Elementary! Women will find any useful object to hold their hair in place, and, in this case, the key! Of which was also one of the most defining differences in this artwork. Jaquet-Droz's doll had hair falling down its back," he explained.

"It's so simple. Might we give it a go?"

"Very well, take a seat!" He put the key into the slot and began to wind up the automaton. Moments later, he, too, was sitting in his chair, and we could hear the gears inside beginning to click and whirl. The doll began to move, its fingers tapping the piano keys, playing a lovely tune. I smiled, entertained by this incredible piece of ingenuity; however, upon looking over at Holmes, his face was distorted.

"Holmes! What's the problem?" I asked. "This is marvellous, but you look horrified." Suddenly, Sherlock Holmes stood up, grabbed my arm tightly, and pulled me out of my chair.

"Move! Fast!" he yelled. I stood to my feet, and he pushed me into his room, dashing in behind me and slamming the door.

"What in the name of…" but I was cut short as I realised what had happened.

A great explosion rattled all of 221B Baker Street. A hole was blown in the wall of Holmes's room. Pictures and trinkets fell from the walls and tables. I was dazed and, to my right, Holmes lay beside me, eyes closed and unmoving. I stood to my feet and wobbled to the door. The study was in shambles, and where the doll once sat, an empty shell remained. Its intent was now clear; we were lucky to be alive.

"Watson… where are you?" came Holmes's faint voice. I darted over to him, took his pulse, and checked his eyes. He was fine, just shaken.

"Holmes! You saved us both!" I exclaimed.

"I'm sorry for being so forceful with you, my dear Watson, but there was no time to discuss the matter."

"I am grateful that you didn't waste any time." I picked Holmes up from the floor and, with his arm around me, we stepped back into the study to examine the damage. Pieces of the automaton lay scattered around the room, and our books and papers were in an unbelievable mess. "Let me check on Mrs Hudson." I left Holmes to stand on his own as I searched for our landlady. Heaven forbid anything happen to her. "Baker Street without dear Mrs Hudson; England would fall!" I thought to myself.

Looking into the hallway, there was no sign of her. I flew down the stairs, calling out to her. To my great relief, I found Mrs Hudson alive in the kitchen, curled in a ball on the floor. "Are you all right?" I asked, reaching out to her.

"Oh, Doctor, what happened?" Mrs Hudson asked in a shaken tone.

"Seems someone tried to kill Holmes and possibly me."

"Are you both uninjured?"

"We are. However, the rooms are a mess. I left Holmes upstairs. You stay here while we sort it." She nodded. I found Holmes rummaging through the wreckage. "What are you doing?"

"Looking for clues! If you know anything about art, you'll know that even in a recreation, the artist will find some subtle way to leave their mark. I won't take this lightly, Watson. Not only were you, my friend, put in danger, but complete strangers could have died had this explosion been any bigger. The fact that it wasn't means it was intended for me!"

"Or us," I remarked.

"Watson, as valuable as you are as my companion and chronicler, you are of no threat to the criminals that operate within this city. Killing you would only be an addition to the number of bodies, not a commendable success for them."

"Holmes!" I roared, irritated by this cold remark. "Does this have anything to do with the letter you received a while ago, after our return from Morfa Nefyn?" Holmes stood emotionless and in silence. "I know you, Holmes, you didn't stop looking into the matter."

"I couldn't leave it alone, Watson! The only risk, I thought, was to my own life. I am truly sorry for the threat upon your life, my friend." I saw true sorrow on his face. It was one of the rare moments when his guard went down and revealed a more vulnerable side. "Hello there!" He suddenly bent over and picked up a small fragment that looked like a piece of the automaton. "Watson, come see this," he held his glass to the portion of burnt wood which sported a bit of writing.

"I can barely read this, Holmes." He began to rub the blackness away as best he could.

"It says: Al Pievel Romontsch… Stai si, Defenda… Risguard Pretenda… patraty," read Holmes.

"I'm not familiar with this," I muttered.

"It's Romansh; spoken in Switzerland. It says: To the Romansh people... Stand up, Defend... Demand Respect... thought."

"That hardly makes any sense to me!"

"It's a poem written by Giachen Caspar Muoth, a Swiss man. So tell me, Watson, what can you deduce?"

"Pardon?"

"We are meant to be dead. Thankfully, we are not, so we have the upper hand. We must seize this opportunity to find our attacker. This poem is our clue. We are looking for an exceptional Swiss clockmaker within the city," he said vibrantly, as if there was no effect from our near-death experience.

"Within the city? How can you be so sure?"

"Observe. What were the papers that packed the box? They were *Daily News, The Times, The Evening Journal,* and *The Daily Telegraph,* as well as an assortment of flyers and local advertisements. It seems obvious that whoever packed it was local. Now, I know what you're thinking: someone could have sent the mechanical doll from elsewhere, had it repacked, and sent it to us as a diversion; however, looking closely at the explosion, I can detect the usage of the British-made chemical, lyddite. It is a type of chemical resembling picric acid, which, as you should know, Watson, has been used for various military purposes. Something else I am certain of: the maker of such a machine, though created for destruction, would not let someone else tinker with it by putting a bomb inside. Nay, they would have to do it themselves."

"I'm still not sure how we can find the man or how you know he is Swiss."

146

"Romansh, Watson. The creator inscribed a Swiss poem written in Romansh. The poem itself says:

'To the Romansh People.
Stand up, Defend,
Romansh, Your Old Language,
Demand Respect,
For your thought.'

"This is a patriotic poem; only someone from this background would use such a vivid piece of writing. The artist has a strong connection to this language, most likely they are from the Graubunden region of Switzerland, where it is heavily spoken," said Holmes.

"Outstanding!" I shouted. "So, surely we must be off. I would believe that a man of such artistic reputation would be known, especially among the other clockmaker-makers in the city."

"Capital, Watson! I agree, a clock-maker would be our best choice, and I think I know the perfect place to start." As we prepared to leave, I could hear a commotion outside. I looked out our window, and a crowd of people had gathered. I hadn't taken a moment to think of the public outside and how things must look to them. I could see several police officers coming from Oxford Street. One officer pushed the door open and came upstairs.

"Halloa!" he cried.

"We are in here, Officer," Holmes called casually.

"Mr Holmes? Ah, thank heavens. It's good to see you are well," the officer gasped, his hat tilting forward over his eyes. "What happened here?"

"We received a package with an automaton inside. It exploded and nearly killed us," said I. "Fortunately, Holmes was one step ahead and saved our lives."

"It was really quite simple, though. The doll was playing a melody clearly designed to cover up the noise of the malfunctioning gears working to detonate the explosive. Though, from your expression, Watson, you missed the clue. As it played, I noticed a distinct clicking noise that was out of time with the other gears, then I caught a whiff of a toxic aroma that escaped as the gears warmed up. It was a simple deduction that this odd noise was no mistake and was meant to conclude terminally."

"It would have been a great blow to the world if we had lost you!" the officer assured.

"You pay me a strong compliment, officer," said Holmes, "but I am glad to be alive. Now, my good man, do us a grand service. We are on our way out following a fresh lead; keep our fate a secret for now. It could be helpful to work under the disguise of death."

"Will do, Mr Holmes!"

"Come, Watson. We can leave out the back!"

"I'm right behind you!" said I, following Holmes down the back stairs and out the door. We rushed through alleys for some time until we reached Marylebone High Street, where we jumped into a hansom, and Holmes shouted, "Zingre & Co. on Cheapside. There will surely be a generous tip if you make great haste!"

Five-One-Eight-One-Eight-Nine-Nine

As we splashed down the cobbled street, Holmes and I held tight for fear of being tumbled around within the compartment. Without warning, we took a sharp turn down Oxford Street, which felt as if the wheels stood on end as we were thrust to one side.

The driver disregarded all courtesy as he raced along the streets. I observed a heavy concentration of people ahead of us, near Tottenham Court Road, which he avoided by turning and dashing past Soho Square and coming out on Shaftesbury Avenue.

The hansom made another sharp turn and burst through the Seven Dials; I could hear women yelling and burly men shouting obscenities as we disrupted the flow. We came out on Newgate Street, and I could see the dome of St Paul's Cathedral in the distance. With a sudden jerk, the hansom stopped, throwing us forward. We had arrived at our destination. Holmes and I stepped out and found ourselves at Zingre and Co. As I gathered myself, Holmes paid the driver.

"Well done, my good man. Would you stay and wait for us? We are in urgent need of a well-handled driver such as you."

"Thank you, Mister. With payment this good, I'll be here a'waitin'!" Holmes shook the driver's hand, sealing their verbal agreement. He turned, tapping me on the arm as he walked towards the entrance to the small clockmaker's shop.

Zingre and Co. was not a well-known business; in fact, had it been known to anyone other than Holmes, I would have been surprised. It rested between two other shops and seemed little more than a divider between them.

Holmes and I entered the narrow shop, and a tiny bell jingled as the door opened. The walls on both sides were filled with clocks, wind-up dolls, and music boxes.

Behind a counter, towards the back of the shop, sat a man whom I placed at six-and-thirty years of age. He was bent over with two small instruments in his hands, tinkering with an open fob watch. He wore a pair of binocular glasses as he worked on the intricate pieces. We approached the counter.

"I'll be with you in a moment," said the man, not bothering to look up. After a small clicking noise, the man straightened, took off his glasses, and looked at us both. "What can I do for you, gentlemen?" I detected a European accent, which was clearly mixed with many years of living in England. Holmes put his hand on the counter and laid out several pieces from the exploded automaton.

"My good man, I am Mr Sherlock Holmes, and this is my colleague, Doctor John Watson. We had a unique gift come to us today, an automaton. It was a woman playing a piano, modelled after Jaquet-Droz. I was hoping you could lead us in the direction of its maker."

"Why do you assume I know its creator?" asked the clockmaker. "There are plenty of very talented makers in the city."

"Because these gears were purchased at your shop," said Holmes, turning one of them over to reveal the initials Z&CO. "You, like all artists, want credit for your work. Now, I know that, at some point, you sold items to a fellow Swiss man; someone of exceedingly high talent and of Romansh background. As a Swiss man yourself, it should not be hard to place a man like that," said Holmes definitively. The shopkeeper stood motionless. Holmes stared at him intensely, and he stared back. It was a battle to see who would break under the pressure. Finally, Holmes blinked and loosened his form. "If you will not co-operate, I will be left with no other choice but to involve the authorities, and they will not share the same care and respect that I show." He turned and began to walk out. As he put his hand on the door, the clockmaker stopped us.

"Mr Holmes, wait." We both turned and walked back to the counter. "I know who it is. But he isn't easily found. His name is Jetmir Von Gunten. He came in here about a month ago and said he needed equipment for something he was building. I asked where his shop was, and he refused to tell me, saying that's not what he does. He just wanted supplies and didn't have time to wait for a shipment to come in. I was reluctant at first, but he asked, as a Swiss man, for my help specifically. He then offered me a thousand pounds for gears and sorts that wouldn't have cost but a hundred pounds. I took the money and gave him free rein of my inventory. He didn't take much, but some of what he did take included my personalised gears, which you have now found."

"Do you know where we might find him?" I asked. "Has he had you send anything to him?"

"As a matter of fact, he did. He sent me a letter asking me to send him another bundle of gears. He gave me a post office to send the parcel to, but no direct address," he finished.

"Well done. Give us the location of the post office, and we shall be out of your way," said Holmes.

"It was the post office in Stepney," the clockmaker replied.

"Capital! We must be off at once. Thank you for your time," Holmes shouted over his shoulder as we raced out the door and leapt into the hansom waiting for us. Holmes shouted to the driver where to take us next, and we were off.

*****

We pulled up to the post office and went inside. There was a line of people before us, sending and receiving messages of all sorts. Finally, a man behind the counter greeted us. "Sir, I need your assistance," said Holmes. "I need you to tell me where I can find Jetmir Von Gunten. A Swiss man."

"Oh, Mr Von Gunten! He came in the other day and asked us to forward all mail back to Switzerland. Said it was urgent," the man informed us.

"When did he do this?" I asked.

"He came in yesterday," he replied.

"Tell me the last address you had for him," Holmes pressed urgently.

"Oh, all right then. Though I expect you won't find him there," he said as he pulled out the directory. He mumbled to himself as he scrolled through the list. "Ah, it's 5 North Street." The moment he told us, Holmes was turned, heading out the door. I met him in the hansom, and we shot off again. "Mister," said the driver, coming to a stop. "We're a few streets away, just walk up there; I ain't driving my cab that way. I'll wait for you here. It's too rough."

"Very well. We'll return shortly," said Holmes, and we hopped out.

*****

We stood before a rundown storefront. The windows were boarded up and the glass broken. I tried the front door, but it wouldn't move.

"It's locked, Holmes," said I.

"Never mind that, keep an eye out," Holmes retorted. He dropped to the ground and unrolled his leather kit. He pulled out a skeleton key and began working on the lock. Moments later, it clicked. Holmes pushed the door, but it still didn't budge. "Of course, bolted from inside," he mumbled as he walked to the edge of the pavement.

"Shall we go around the back?" I asked.

Then, like a bullet, Holmes lunged at the door, snapping the wood and leaving it swaying on a broken hinge.

"Just as well," said I, and entered.

Inside was a hallway with a staircase to the left and a door on the right that led to an abandoned workshop, and at the end of the hall, what looked like a door leading out the back.

"Perhaps he did leave. There doesn't seem to be any sign of life."

As we walked around what would have been the shop room, all we could find were empty jars, a few broken fob watches, and some gears sprinkled over the floor.

"Watson, you check the cellar while I head upstairs," said Holmes as we stepped back into the hallway.

"Cellar?" I asked.

"Even you should have observed the echoing noise as we walked in, indicating a very large gap between the floors we walked on and the ground underneath. Furthermore, there is a faint aroma of damp, clearly from a low, cold place. A cellar," said Holmes.

"How could I have missed it?"

"You missed it because you were not looking for it," he replied.

"And you were?" I asked.

"I am always looking, Watson. Come, let us not waste any more time." He went up the stairs and I continued down the hall. I opened a door at the end, but all I found was a kitchen. I could see no doorway leading below. I stepped back into the hall and noticed a door underneath the staircase. Disappointingly, when I opened it, I found only a small closet.

"There's a hatch in the floor," called Holmes.

I looked down and noticed a very small black handle. I lifted it, and there was a flight of stairs leading below the house. I slowly descended into the darkness, overwhelmed by a horrid stench. Something brushed across my face, sending a chill down my spine.

Grabbing it, I discovered it was a string. I pulled it, and a small bulb lit up. A soft yellow light illuminated a small circular patch of the cellar. Continuing down, I had a fright when I saw a small pale face with empty eyes staring straight at me.

It looked like a haunted child; soulless and void. When I composed myself, I realised it was nothing more than an automaton. Walking around, I saw that this was where Von Gunten had attempted several different automata and tested multiple types of explosives on them. Underneath his work counter were the remains of the materials used to create the explosive that went off in Baker Street. Suddenly, another fright befell me when I heard a crash behind me.

I turned, my heart racing, as I scanned the area. I calmed when I saw a rat walking about the floor. I had not recalled ever being so on edge as when I was in that cellar. I saw a flyer sitting on the counter. It was announcing a magic and wonders show featuring a man called The Great Antos at the Royal Albert Hall.

There was a sketch of the man, Antos, with a floating chair and several wooden doll faces. For a moment, I thought I could hear the faint sound of breathing.

"Is anyone there?" I called, but got no reply.

Assuming it was my own senses playing a trick, I continued to look around. Then, unmistakably, I heard someone whisper "get… out…"

My pulse doubled, and I called again,

"Show yourself!"

There was a loud bang, the undeniable boom of a revolver being fired, and the light went out. I turned, but my eyes had not yet adjusted to the darkness. Another bang went off, and I flinched at the sound. I saw a spark light up, and the revolver fired a third time; and, for that moment, I saw the face of a man lit up against the black. It was as if I saw the devil himself! The face was pure evil; sinister and vile as it watched me.

"Who are you?" I demanded, trying to feel around for anything I could use as a weapon.

Another shot, and I tucked my head into my arms. I dropped down and hid under the work table, with several discarded automaton parts. I tossed them to one side of the room. When they hit the ground, the gun lit up, and I could see the man's position. The only light I could see was flooding in from the hatch at the top of the stairs. I saw the figure pass in front of it and fade back into the darkness.

The man was making an animal-like growling noise as he lurked. I could hear him reloading his gun in the darkness. I took the risk and ran as fast as I could up the stairs. A shot was fired, and I fell at the noise. I continued up the stairs when a hand grabbed my heel.

Turning, I saw the wicked man trying to pull me down. His eyes were wide and crazed, he foamed at the mouth, and his hair was dishevelled. I kicked him, and he fell back. I continued scrambling out of the cellar, but my assailant was right behind me. He leapt out of the dark cellar and lunged at me with a knife in his hand. It took tremendous effort to hold back his arm. There was a commotion, and suddenly, the man fell unconscious.

The body was lifted off me, and there stood Holmes holding a metal rod.

"Thank you, Holmes," said I, panting.

"Are you all right?" he asked with a concerned expression on his face.

"I am," I acknowledged. "This fiend was hiding down below. Who is he?"

"I reckon he's Von Gunten," remarked Holmes. We restrained the man, binding his hands and feet. As we did so, I could see a curious expression upon my friend's face. Several times, he'd deeply inhale, smelling the air. I, too, noticed this aroma.

"What is this strange odour?" Holmes mumbled.

"Yes, it overpowered me when I went into the cellar."

"It's a curious one," Holmes observed. "And look! It would seem our man has been in a brawl. The bruising and dried blood aren't but a day old."

"Ah!" roared the man in a sudden burst. "Untie me! I've done the work, let me go!" Holmes and I were both startled by this particular reaction. "D-d-did he send you? I bet he did. Tell him I'm done, I'm through! No m-m-more!"

"Von Gunten, calm down!" said Holmes. "If you help us, we can help you."

"Help me? You ca-can't help me!"

"We know you built the automaton that was sent to Baker Street," said Holmes.

Von Gunten looked at us intensely.

"Oh no, it's you! You are Sherlock Holmes, aren't you?! I am most certainly a dead man if you are alive."

"Why did you attack us?"

"I, I was forced to, Mr Holmes. It wasn't a thing I wanted to do."

"Who made you do it then?" I asked.

"The man with the scar. He only goes by the name Azael."

"What does he look like?" Holmes asked.

"A tall, thin man. Bald with, like I said, a scar upon his face. The left side. A gross wound, probably some kind of knife injury, I would think."

"Who is he and why did he have you create these automatons?" Holmes pressed.

"I don't know who he is exactly. He just came to me one day, said he needed a watch fixed; he didn't want to take it to a big shop. That is when everything went out of control. I offered to fix it, and he gave me a generous tip for my work. He was so very pleased with it that he started coming back to me more often for more jobs. I don't even own a shop, so I had to get what I needed from other shops around the city. As a reward, he said he wanted to treat me. I was to meet him at 27 Linchfield, so I did. When I arrived, we went inside and were greeted by a Frenchman, who was making some kind of bargain with a Russian."

"What did the Russian man look like?" Holmes asked.

"The Russian? Not sure, tall, dark hair. I think he was military because he held a jacket with lots of medals on it."

"Most intriguing; please continue," said Holmes.

"Well, the Frenchman showed me into a room, and he showed me a catalogue of women; he said any could be mine. I'm a married man, Mr Holmes, but it would be a lie to say that I am happy in this partnership, so I accepted. The next day, he came to see me and asked if I enjoyed myself. I told him I did, and we agreed that as long as I worked for him, he'd pay for me to use the services there. Then, one day, it was suddenly shut down and gone. That's when Azael came to me and asked me to build him two automata. He gave me the money, and I got the supplies. The next day, he came and said to make them into explosives! I started to refuse, but then he laid down a picture of a woman whom I'd slept with and me. He said she was killed and that if I didn't do his bidding, he'd make it clear I had killed her, but not before exposing me to my wife. He said if I built them, he'd let me go. I ordered my wife to return to Switzerland in hopes of keeping her safe while I did as Azael asked. I built the two automata. One of them I was to deliver to Baker Street, the other I was to wait for Azael to come and collect it," Von Gunten said.

"Given the current state in which we found you, this Azael clearly didn't hold to his end of the bargain," I commented.

"No, he came in just after I returned from delivering the package to Baker Street, and he said he wanted more. I told him no and that our deal was done. He beat me, Mr Holmes, and before I could fight back, he released a devilish gas that knocked me out. When I woke, I was locked in the cellar, and when I heard you open the hatch, I assumed it was Azael or one of his men, so I attacked."

"Where is the other automaton? Where is it meant to explode?" Holmes demanded.

"No, not a bomb, this one was my special work. They wanted it to excrete fumes when it was working and appear to be breathing."

"Breath?" mumbled Holmes. "Of course! Watson, I know what it is I smell!"

"What is it?" I asked.

"The devil's foot!" he exclaimed, standing and pacing about the room. "A similar compound, which was used on Mrs Dabish. It has been used, in a smaller dose, on Von Gunten here to knock him out."

"That explains the awful stench down in the cellar, then!" I exclaimed.

"Von Gunten, you are a part of a bigger scheme. Watson, remember that Dr Dabish spoke of his grand plan and said the world will burn. If you remember, Mrs Dabish mentioned a man with a scar on the left side of his face in her diary, and now Von Gunten is being blackmailed by a man with a scar in a similar place," said Holmes. "Whoever this Azael is, he has the weaponised gas and is planning an attack that will shake the empire! But the question is, what event are they planning to use for their attack?"

"I think I know!" I cried and ran back down into the cellar. I raced back up and handed Holmes the flyer featuring "The Great Antos".

"What is this?" Holmes asked, showing Von Gunten.

"I've not seen this. I recall Azael put something on the table just before he attacked me."

"The Great Antos. He's a prestigious magician known around the world. Part of his acts feature automata! This is most telling, Watson. I now recall that several Russian and German politicians were meant to be attending this event, along with members of the Royal Family," remembered Holmes. "When is it? Oh yes, here's the date, the eighteenth of May at seven o'clock. That's tonight! Watson, what's the time?"

"Six o'clock," I confirmed. He suddenly paused and put his hand on his head, rubbing gently. "I've been so slow, Watson. For months, the word has been slipping out to me, but I've not made the connection. Five-One-Eight-One-Eight-Nine-Nine, yes, it's so clear now!" he exclaimed. "Mrs Dabish knew all along! She knew this was coming! Dr Dabish created the toxin, and she discovered something more than the affair. Something was to happen on five-eighteen-eighteen-ninety-nine! She's American, remember, and that is the American style of dating, but in her psychotic break, she remembered it as one long number. Porlock too, he tried to tell us, May 18, but 'May 18' could have referred to a person and age; without more detail, it was nearly impossible to work out. We don't have much time. This is the perfect place for a public attack. With the current climate in Europe, each country would blame the other, and mark my words, if it succeeds, there will be war!" Holmes concluded.

"And the attack today, it conveniently followed the threatening letter you received a few weeks ago. You must have been hot on their tracks for them to attempt to take us out before we could stop this event tonight!" said I.

"Indeed, Watson, I am hot on their tracks! Come, we don't have much time at all. Von Gunten, I'm sorry, but you must come with us. We need to make great haste to the Royal Albert Hall."

Holmes, Von Gunten, and I quickly departed and made our way towards where our hansom awaited. I could see on Holmes's face that he was greatly angered with himself. For months, he had been chasing loose ends, attempting to understand whatever grand scheme was at play, only to turn up with nothing; yet, clear as day, the clues were in front of us the entire time. Holmes had been given vague hints, but nothing solid enough to lead him anywhere, and now time was against us. The finale was now less than an hour away, and it would be no easy task getting from North Street to the Royal Albert Hall in Kennington. When our hansom driver saw us running up with Von Gunten, he jumped off his perch and blocked our entrance.

"What's happened here?" he asked.

"This man is in our custody. He must come with us," said Holmes. "We will need you to get us to the Royal Albert Hall as fast as possible!" We tried to get into the hansom again, but the driver continued to deny us.

"What I mean is, what's happened here?" The driver held up the evening paper. The headline read: SHERLOCK HOLMES & DOCTOR JOHN WATSON: KILLED IN BAKER STREET BOMBING?

"This is you two," he said, pointing to our photographs. Though it should be said that Holmes's image was a blur next to a very clear image of myself. Holmes could rarely be found in a photograph.

"Well, it seems our disguise has worked thus far!" Holmes admitted. "My apologies, my good man, for this fright. We are not the living dead; we are merely using a timely diversion."

"I don't want to be pulled into some mess, you see," said the driver adamantly.

"Let me explain," I interjected. "We were, in fact, attacked this morning, but we escaped the blast. You are only one of a few persons in all of London to know this story to be false."

"You are helping me on the most important case of the year!" affirmed Holmes with a smile. The driver looked at us for some time.

"Let's get you to the Royal Albert Hall then," he returned, breaking the silence. "I'm sorry, but it was just a fright to see you both dead in the paper but alive in my cab. I'm honoured to be a part of one of your adventures, Mr Holmes. Get in!" he said with a wretched smile. I was suddenly nervous to step back into the hansom. We let Von Gunten in first, then Holmes tapped me on the shoulder and motioned for me to follow. I heard the crack of the whip and the driver yell at his horse, and with a great jerk, we were off.

*****

"Keep it steady!" I yelled. It was difficult enough to keep myself from being tossed around the compartment, let alone keep from crushing the other occupants. Holmes smirked at my restlessness as we dashed down streets, causing havoc everywhere we turned. I could hear the sound of street vendors and pedestrians shouting in protest once more as we blazed down the cobbled roads.

"We've got company!" yelled the driver.

"What do you mean?" I pressed.

"We've been followed," said Holmes. "Someone must have been watching Von Gunten." I turned and looked behind us, but saw nothing. Suddenly, the entire compartment shook as something collided with the side opposite me. I was nearly pushed through the window of the hansom as a result. I turned and saw the rogue driver who assaulted us.

"Keep calm! I'll try to lose them!" shouted our driver.

He took a sharp turn down an alley which was barely large enough for the hansom. We burst out onto a busy street, knocking over a vegetable stand.

"They are still behind us!" Holmes announced.

"They've got more power! Two horses to my one!" replied the driver. He whipped the horse several more times to pick up speed. "I'll lose them in the water."

"What do you mean?" I cried.

We made another sharp turn, and I could see the Thames in the distance. Our driver aimed right for it. Carts and cabs parted as we roared down the road. Police whistles streamed past, but nothing would stop us. I heard several shots, and we ducked as bullets ripped through the back of our hansom.

Then, we made a hard turn. I could see the Thames and feared that we were about to fall into it. Holmes, Von Gunten, and I pushed to the left, and the hansom straightened. I looked behind and saw the pursuing vehicles attempt to avoid the water, but their horses were moving with such force that they could not make the turn in time, and they crashed into the water.

"Aha! We got them!" shouted the driver. Then, out of nowhere, another cab burst out of an alley and slammed into us.

"Holmes, get down!" I shouted as I saw an arm reach out of the parallel cab, extending a gun.

The man inside fired several shots, and one bullet grazed my arm. Another shot was fired, and I saw our driver fall from his seat. The horse, now terribly spooked, went out of control. Our hansom tipped sharply to one side and flipped over. The three of us inside the compartment fell painfully over each other as the horse dragged the tipped hansom several yards before finally stopping.

I shoved Von Gunten off me and called out, "Is everyone alive?"

"I am. How are you both?" Holmes replied.

"I've been grazed by a bullet, and my head is pounding, but nothing more," I returned.

"I'm alive, too," said Von Gunten in a shaky tone.

"Let's get out of here," said Holmes.

We crawled out of the shattered hansom and reached down to help pull Von Gunten to his feet. As I helped him up, a black cab strode past and fired four shots, each into Von Gunten's back. He let out a cry of pain and fell into me. The cab sped off, and I laid him gently on the ground. The people around us were screaming and running in fear. Holmes and I stood over Von Gunten; he gargled, and blood trickled from his mouth. I checked his pulse as it quickly faded, then sat, with my knees in my chest, on the pavement.

"This is a dangerous game, Watson. Whoever these people are, they have succeeded in two things: killing off a key witness and learning that we are not dead."

We heard a police officer's whistle and saw one running around the corner. He marvelled at the destruction before him. Holmes and I stood and greeted the man.

"I'm Mr Sherlock Holmes."

"Oh yes, I know who you are. How are you not dead?"

"Sorry to disappoint you," said Holmes, "and you are?"

"I'm Officer Barnes. I heard the explosion at Baker Street was a big 'un, but clearly you are both fine," he said. "Are you hurt from the accident?"

"A little shaken, but we will be fine. More importantly, we have had a few casualties: our cab driver and this man here, both shot down by an unknown figure in a black hansom," I informed.

"It's not a lot to go on, is it?" remarked Officer Barnes.

"Unfortunately, it is not," agreed Holmes.

"Who is this man?" the officer asked, bending down and looking at Von Gunten's lifeless body.

"His name is Jetmir Von Gunten, a Swiss man who lived on North Street. He tinkered with clockworks and was a remarkable artist; dark powers manipulated him," Holmes quickly told.

"Where were you going?" Officer Barnes pressed.

"To Albert Hall; I'm urgently needed there," Holmes stated.

"What's the problem?" he asked.

"We think there will be an attack," I admitted.

"At Albert Hall?" questioned Officer Barnes unbelievingly. "There's a big event going on there tonight; the Royals and foreign diplomats will be there."

"Indeed, which means we must leave you now. The show begins in just twenty-five minutes. We must avert the plan that is in motion," Holmes said sternly.

"Come on then, leave this mess with me. Let us get you a cab!" We stepped into another hansom, and Officer Barnes instructed the driver where to take us, informing him that it was urgent police business and to make great haste.

*****

As we sat in the new hansom, I could feel my muscles aching and the wound in my arm becoming increasingly tender. The fresh glow of newly ignited street lamps splashed light into our dark compartment. I admit that I felt defeated by this point. My mind fell back to our poor driver who had been shot. I regret that I have no recollection of his name. He offered his life in service to the greater good, to justice. I could tell by Holmes's expression that his mind was only focused on reaching the Hall. The losses we suffered would catch up later. This moment was about preventing additional loss of life.

We rode through Trafalgar Square and down The Mall towards Buckingham Palace. Not far in the distance stood the Royal Albert Hall. It was lit up in splendour. The street was flooded with cabs and people running in the gently falling rain. The time was ten past seven, and the show had already begun. We had little time to find a way inside and locate the second fatal automaton before it was able to fulfil its purpose.

"You can stop here," Holmes told the driver when we were but a moment's walk from the main door.

"I was told to take you around the back. Officer's orders," informed the driver.

"Never mind them. Let us out here," Holmes repeated demandingly. The driver did not listen; he continued around the bend at Kensington Gore and stopped.

"Why stop us here?" I asked. "You've only set us back!"

"Watson," Holmes warned. I looked at him in confusion.

"You can't be allowed to continue, Mr Holmes," said the driver. Looking at him, I saw that he held a revolver in his hand.

"Barnes—he is one of you, your man on the inside," Holmes realised.

"Elementary guess, Mr Holmes," sneered the driver.

"Not a guess. An observation of the facts. Barnes didn't hide his disappointed reaction to our survival. He showed more concern that we survived than for the dead man at our feet," recalled Holmes.

"Well done, well done, indeed. But you fell right into his trick nevertheless, and now you'll just be one of the first casualties of this great war."

"Sadly, no," said Holmes, who quickly lunged at the man and bent his arm upwards. I reached out and took the gun from his hands while Holmes held his throat until he fell unconscious. Holmes pulled the driver out and dragged him over to an iron fence, where he cuffed our attacker's hands to it. "Come, Watson, no more of this nonsense."

*****

Holmes and I walked around the front of the Royal Albert Hall. Our apparel was nothing to marvel at; we were dishevelled, dirty, and now wet from the rainfall. We received many unpleasant glances from those mingling outside the main door. Holmes passed the doorman a couple of ten-pound notes, and he let us in with no trouble. As we entered, we could hear the show. Crowds were 'awing' at the magician's tricks. We walked up the stairs to get a view from the top; the entire hall was packed. I could see the Russian and German political powers seated next to the English royals down front. They were in perfect positions for an attack from the stage. Holmes leaned over and asked a woman for her evening's programme, which she reluctantly handed over.

"Look, Watson," Holmes whispered. "The event is to be over by ten past eight. We've got twenty minutes. Ah, and look, there is even a warning here that this show will use pyrotechnics and fire effects. It'll look like an accident, but you can guarantee some conveniently placed evidence will be found after the deed is done."

"I suspect you are correct!" I agreed.

"Come, we don't have much time," said Holmes.

"And now! For my finale, I will speak to the dead! Assistants, if you please," announced Antos. Someone pulled a large lever off to the side, and an automaton rose from the stage in a cloud of smoke. It sat on a box, dressed as a workhouse boy. One of Antos's assistants walked out onto the stage and handed him a small chalkboard and a pointing stick, which were placed next to the automaton.

"This is it!" said I.

"The gas will be underneath, and they'll channel it up. Watson, we cannot allow him to activate the automaton!" cried Holmes.

"My automaton is no ordinary one! Through him, the dead can speak, and you can even feel their breath envelope the room!" Antos continued. "I will need some volunteers; how about we bring up some very special guests? Admiral Hague and General Fitzory, will you, or your wives, be so kind as to assist me?"

"Hague! Of course! The keyword, Watson!" A sudden realisation stunned Holmes momentarily.

"Look!" I pointed to a man in military dress walking up the aisle. The man said something into Admiral Hague's ear, and he stood up, apologising for not being able to take part. "He's bowing out and leaving the room."

"Of course he is!" roared Holmes. "And he's offered his wife to the slaughter."

"What's his game?" I asked.

"I have a theory, but now is not the time," replied Holmes. "We must get behind the stage." We dashed out of the hall and into the foyer, where we broke through a small crowd of conversing people. An usher, holding the door to backstage, stopped us as we rushed upon him.

"Where do you think you're going?" he asked.

"It is a matter of urgent police business that you let us pass," demanded Holmes.

"Where are your credentials?" he asked.

"Unless you want to be solely responsible for the deaths of every person in that room and the reason the entire world is lit up with war, I strongly insist that you move out of our way!" I exclaimed.

"I'm afraid your tricks won't work on me," he whistled, signalling for a nearby officer to join him.

"I'm afraid this won't do," said Holmes coolly.

He tripped the usher and burst through the door. We found our way backstage, and we could hear several officers following us.

"This way!" called Holmes.

The stage on which Antos performed was elevated to hide many of his trap doors and conceal his illusions. I found the lift where the automaton had risen and saw a man tinkering with an oven-like container that had a series of pipes running into and out of the automaton above.

There was a marvellous gear system that connected the automaton to the container. It appeared to work as a generator, funnelling the gas out into the crowd. The man hooking up the system saw Holmes and me coming towards him. He quickly finished and, like a devil, dashed away. As we rapidly climbed through beams and metal bars to reach the system, we heard Antos bring the automaton to life. Its movements were triggering the gears, which would begin funnelling the gas.

"Watson, stop them!" shouted Holmes.

I saw two officers crawling towards us. One approached me, and I cracked my cane on his head before he could advance any further. While he was unconscious, I took his revolver from his belt and moved to intercept the other officer aiming for Holmes. Up on stage, Antos was letting off loud explosions.

"I'll shoot if you do not stop!" the officer warned Holmes.

Holmes ignored the demand, and the officer took better aim. Suddenly, the officer and I both flinched at the sound of an exceptionally loud pop-up on stage. The audience shouted, then cheered; it was clearly part of the act. As fast as I could, I climbed through to reach the other officer. He saw me and began firing upon me.

I dodged several bullets and called out, "You don't know what you're doing!"

I fired a shot back but made it clear that it was just a warning. I looked for Holmes, but could not see him. Suddenly, a shaft of light came down, and Holmes leapt up through one of the trap doors onto the stage. I heard panicked screaming and Antos yelling. Then I saw the automaton slide down the hole Holmes had just gone up, and the trap door that had opened as the automaton ascended. A hand dropped something down the pipe, which fed into the container, and the trap door closed. A moment later, the container exploded, shaking both the officer and me before my world went dark.

*****

I woke a few moments later to Holmes reviving me. "My dear Watson, I'm terribly sorry; you will be all right, I will not forgive myself otherwise!" He placed me in a chair, and my head spun before everything came back into focus.

"What happened?" I asked.

"Ah, capital! You are responsive. Well, while you were fending off those ridiculous officers, I realised that since the machine was already in motion, there would be no way to stop it in time. The only way to defuse it was to blow it up, so I pulled open a trap door and went onto the stage. As Antos attempted to stop me, I was forced to quickly incapacitate him. I then disposed of the automaton, opened the trap door, took a small explosive, and dropped it into the pipe, which fed into the container holding the fumes. Needless to say, I gave the audience a better finale than they expected."

"Then we've done it!" said I.

"Hardly, we have extensive questioning for multiple suspects ahead of us. Hopefully, we can get behind the veil of this criminal mastery," mused Holmes.

My attention was caught by a bald man standing in the shadows. His face was just barely visible, but I could make out that he had a horrible scar descending from the left eyebrow down to his chin. It looked like an old battle wound, probably from a knife. Was this the man Von Gunten told us of?

"Holmes, behind you, a man with a scar," I whispered. Holmes turned, and the man's eyes widened when he realised Holmes was looking at him.

"Azael!" shouted Holmes.

The man took off. Holmes ran after him, and I followed at a slower pace. My friend dashed out the back entrance. I quickly followed and saw Azael running up Kennington Road. With great haste, we chased after him, but he was fading out of sight. He ran through Kensington Gardens, which, at this time of night, was not easy to navigate. Holmes, however, was like an owl and never seemed to lose sight of the man. When we had nearly reached the opposite side of the Gardens, Azael was some ways ahead, peering in the entrance, trying to see us. Holmes motioned to stop, and we hunched down so as to be less obvious in our approach. Azael held a revolver in his hand and fired a couple of shots into the Gardens before continuing in his escape.

"Come, Watson, he's going to Paddington!" said Holmes, and the chase resumed. We followed him exactly to where Holmes said: Paddington Station. For a moment, we lost him in the crowds, but I caught a quick glimpse of him and indicated to Holmes. We kept a fair distance from Azael, and from his demeanour, he believed he had lost us.

"Come, Holmes, let's get the authorities and arrest him!" I whispered.

"No, look, Watson," Holmes pointed ahead.

I saw Admiral Hague greeting Azael; both looked deeply concerned. They quickly boarded a train destined for Herefordshire, and Holmes nudged me to follow them. As quickly as we possibly could, without making a scene, we made our way to the train. Upon boarding the coach, Holmes cautiously walked up the hall to see where Azael and Hague were located. He found them both sitting in the first compartment of the first-class carriage.

"Shall I get us a couple of tickets?" I asked.

"Never mind that, Watson, I have a pair here," said Holmes.

"By Jove! When did you get them?"

"This morning," he replied.

"You really must explain this, Holmes."

"In time, come, we must hide first." To our luck, we were able to sit in the compartment directly behind the two men. It was unoccupied and all the better to keep an eye on their movements.

"What are we to do?" I asked.

"I intend to follow them to whatever end. It could help unravel this entire operation! Porlock gave us the clue in his keyword."

"But what I don't understand is Hague's connection, and how you knew we'd need this train!"

"Regarding the Admiral, I find it curious that he was willing to let his wife go up on stage and be murdered. He cares for her little, my friend. So the question is, who does he really care for."

"A mistress, clearly," said I. "But it's no strange thing for a man of that calibre to have many mistresses even with a wife at home."

"But, Watson," Holmes interrupted, "it's not every day that the unfaithful man is willing to murder his wife. He's clearly made an alibi, hence his timely departure from the show, which will hold whether his wife is alive or dead. Either way, he would have certainly been in a position to get away free of any suspicion. The fact that we have him now connected with Azael quashes his alibi."

"What about the tickets then, how did you know we'd need this train?" I asked; however, Holmes was deep in thought and paid no further attention to my questions.

*****

The train had been moving for a short while. Holmes and I abandoned our conversation to be on top alert, making sure we knew where the two men were at all times. Holmes instinctively knew when we were about to slow down and call in at a station. When this would happen, he'd motion for me to go stand at the far end of the coach and watch for the men's departure. It wasn't until we reached Worcester Foregate that anything of real interest occurred. I did as usual and waited by the far exit to see if Azael or Hague would depart.

The train came to a jerky halt, and as I stood there, gripping the top of my cane, their compartment door opened. The two men vacated and casually walked across the platform. Holmes came out of our compartment, and we left the train. We followed the two men down some stairs to the main road.

They got a hansom, and we heard Hague say, "Take us to the Petrus Estate." Holmes and I approached another cab and ordered the same destination. The driver looked at us in agitation.

"That's eighteen miles away; boy, ain't no chance of me going all that way at this time of night. Local trips only," returned the driver.

"I assure you the price we are willing to pay will cover any cost of inconvenience," admitted Holmes.

The driver perked up at this. "How much we talking?" he asked.

"Fifty pounds," said Holmes, "and if you wait for us once we arrive, another fifty for our return."

"Good lord! What a fool am I to pass up this offer? Get in, gents," and we were off. A way ahead, we could see the faint yellow glow of Azael and Hague's hansom as they drove up the long dirt road. I could hear Holmes mumbling under his breath, but I was unable to discern what he was saying. I thought it best not to interrupt his deep concentration.

"Petrus, Watson, it is interesting," he said.

"Why is that?" I asked.

"It's Latin for Peer, which, as you know, is Norwegian."

"I am all ears, Holmes, explain."

"Petrus is the entire reason why we are here. It's why I had the tickets. Coming here was inevitable!" said Holmes. "You remember the name on the card which I found on Porlock's body?"

"Of course, it said Peer. You think this Petrus and Peer are related?" I asked.

"I know they are. The strands have been there, but they are now cemented," said Holmes.

"What do you mean?"

"Two hundred years ago, a Norwegian family, of Latin lineage, bearing the surname Petrus, moved to England. Upon settling in Kent, they changed their name to Peer. It was also in Kent where they met an Irish family named Murtag. The two families have had a long history and a bond which they have yet to fully relinquish. There was, however, an incident one hundred years ago which did cause an irrevocable change. Both families were found to be working together in cheating and blackmailing many members of the local town and were forced out. The two families parted ways and changed their names, but their physical separation did not break their bond. Nay, one family moved north and one stayed south. The family down south started a shipping business that was deeply connected to the northern family, as shipments often passed through that area. Everything hinged on their new names. Since the previous life had to be left behind, they needed a new name, but not without completely withdrawing from their roots. About seventy years ago, the new names became concrete. Murtag became Moriarty and Peer became Perny."

"Professor James Moriarty and Doctor Jotham Perny!" I exclaimed.

"These two families have been building up a vast criminal empire, with Moriarty leading the way—a legacy that is a 'force to be reckoned with', if you will!"

"But both men are dead!"

"Do you believe everything you read in the papers, my dear Watson? How many times must I tell you the official reports cannot always be trusted?"

"So, you think Perny has reverted to his ancient family name of Petrus and continued his criminal reign under the organisational name of Peer?"

"Is it all so out of the question, Watson?"

"Mister, this is a private drive," the driver interjected. "I can tell you are in risky business, what with offering me so much money, but for my own safety, I must let you off here. The estate is right up this lane."

Holmes smirked. "You've done marvellously. Wait around here. It may do you some good to conceal yourself, though. Watch for our return," said Holmes, handing the driver the money as promised.

*****

We slowly crept up the dark wooded path. The glow from Azael and Hague's carriage was returning. Holmes and I ducked into a bush to hide ourselves as the horse and cart rolled past. We waited till it reached the main road before we continued up the way. Finally, we came to a large iron gate that rose some eight feet into the air. Surrounding the inner property was a seven-foot brick wall. I could see the house with several lights shining from the first and second floors.

"My word, Holmes, this is a fortress!"

"It would have to be," he replied.

"Right this way, Mr Holmes," a deep, menacing voice came from the darkness. The massive iron gate opened, and we could see a butler standing in the night air. "They await you inside." The man walked off, and Holmes and I both followed.

"Wait here," the butler instructed as we stood in the main entryway of the mansion. He walked up a curved staircase to the second floor beyond our sight. Looking around, I noticed that to the right was a large sitting room with a roaring fire and to the left a door leading into a small study which opened into a dining hall.

"Mr Holmes, so good of you to join us," came the voice of someone descending the stairs. It was Azael.

"Mr Azael," Holmes greeted with a nod.

"Please, come this way," said Azael. With a bright smile on his face, he walked past us and into the large sitting room. "Come, please come," he urged. Holmes and I followed, and I took in the grandeur of the room. Large, immaculate paintings hung on the walls with various mounted animal heads above small gold plaques, commemorating hunts. A shiny grand piano sat in one corner, and along two walls were oak bookcases. Azael motioned us to take a seat in front of the fire, which we did. He sat in a chair across from us, grinning from ear to ear.

"We wait here, now," said he.

Moments later, Admiral Hague came through the door, followed by a man who appeared somewhat familiar. I then recalled the photograph that Holmes had shown me in '97. I knew the man's face, but it was much older and extremely thin. His eyes were like a serpent's, black and soulless, and he had thinning hair and a white beard. No matter the reports in the papers, the fact was that Doctor Jotham Perny stood there before us, alive and well. He had achieved what Moriarty could not: a resurrection.

"Mr Holmes," said Doctor Perny gently, "I must commend you for your frivolous actions over the past few months. I can understand why my predecessor became so angry with you every time you foiled his plans. I admit, you have nearly foiled two of my biggest operations, and it is most concerning."

"I cannot say that I am sorry, Doctor," sneered Holmes.

"Well, this was the game I wished to play with you, I suppose. Only now it has gone too far and must come to an end."

"I did inform you that you will not win this game," Holmes replied.

"Well, I seem to have the upper hand, and for that, I shall let you play the next move. Thrill us with your powers of deduction that brought us to this moment!" said Doctor Perny with a laugh. "Please, Mr Holmes, the floor is yours."

"As you wish. Though, let me go back some ways then," said Holmes. "After the incident in '97, at the Diamond Jubilee, when we thwarted your organisations assignation attempt on the Queen, I kept a close eye on you. Your activities calmed while the events blew over. Your partner,

Lars, never spoke a whisper of your name, and naturally, there was nothing substantial to connect you to each other apart from one photograph, which I found, of you and him together with Professor Moriarty. Childhood friends, you were. However, my perspective changed only slightly when I heard of your sudden death. I admit that I did believe that you died, though I never believed the cause was heart failure, like the papers reported. It seemed more likely that someone had finally taken their revenge on you.

"When a card was found on both Porlock and Mr Laurent, saying Peer, I began to have growing concerns as to who and what this was. I then recalled seeing Petrus, a similar form of the name, written in Dabish's laboratory on a piece of parchment. Dabish, of course, was the man you hired to weaponise the devil's-foot root, of which traces were found in Von Gunten's cellar.

"It was not until last month, while in Wales, that I came to the conclusion that Peer was, in fact, a much wider organisation than originally thought, one that the poor Miss Stonewall was frantically trying to cut ties from, to the point of suicide, and to which young Randall Lovett had become horribly entangled. Upon this discovery, I received a threatening letter demanding I withdraw from my actions, but my interest was too piqued. Peer was something that I would not let go of. It was in my research into said name that I came across 'Petrus', the name found in Dabish's laboratory. As I ventured even further down the rabbit hole, I came across an interesting family history between the Moriartys and the Pernys.

"I soon discovered that an old estate belonging to the Peer family had been purchased and its name changed to Petrus; the coincidence was too obvious. That is when your death looked more like a fabrication than a fact. Therefore, I had full intentions of coming out to the estate, but those plans were put on hold.

"You knew I was getting closer, and as I continued looking into Petrus, you decided to take Doctor Watson and me out of the equation. You seized the opportunity to have Von Gunten create two weapons, one for me, and one for the Albert Hall. When the attack on Baker Street failed, I was able to trace everything to Von Gunten, and it all snapped perfectly into place; the end of the puzzle. He told us everything he knew, which led me to the Albert Hall, where for months, rumours of this attack had slipped out. It was you, Perny, who hired Dabish to create a weaponised toxin made from the devil's foot root. It was you who killed Porlock because you discovered he was feeding me information about 'May 18.' Your funding came from various sources, such as the gambling ring which trapped the Lovett family. Once they were hooked into your gambling ring, you sent Miss Stonewall to bleed them dry, but that is not all. You worked with Mr Laurent, who ran a private brothel at 27 Linchfield. It was here that Admiral Hague purchased himself a mistress."

"How the hell do you know that?!" burst the Admiral, with rage burning in his eyes.

"Ah, now, now, Admiral, let Mr Holmes finish," Doctor Perny gently scolded and let Holmes continue.

"The first clue of your involvement, Admiral, was Porlock and the use of your name to decipher his message. Then, Von Gunten spoke of the Russian military man who was bartering for one of the girls at the brothel. All of this solidified when I saw you tonight at the Albert Hall and how you quickly left the room just before the final act with a cleverly timed alibi. I must say, an attack like you had planned for tonight would have surely erupted in all-out war, not to mention rid you of your wife."

"Well done! Mr Holmes! Well done indeed!" cheered Doctor Perny, mockingly.

Azael, who was still sitting, began to clap his hands. I glanced at Holmes, and he turned to look at me. Suddenly, Admiral Hague fell to the floor with a bullet in his head. Both Holmes and I were stunned at this utterly random act. Doctor Perny stood grinning, holding the smoking gun.

"Now, Mr Holmes," said Doctor Perny, "despite your foiling my plans so many times, I've come up with another. The headlines will read: World Famous Detective Murders Russian Admiral At Request of Brother's Wish."

"No one would believe such nonsense!" I cried.

"When they find you and Holmes with bullets lodged in your skulls, a signed letter from dear brother Mycroft will be found tucked away in 221b Baker Street, and nicely placed documents within Mycroft Holmes's office; it'll be clear. Besides, isn't it always your opinion, Mr Holmes, that the headlines cannot be trusted? It is but a minor thing to manipulate the media these days. Admiral Hague's death is an unfortunate loss, but there is always collateral damage. It was always part of the plan; it will spark the war."

"And tell me, how do you come out on top?" asked Holmes.

"Mr Holmes, my, my, you have missed the point. Not everything is about capital gain! Of course, it was capital gain that fuelled Moriarty! Not me, though. I just like to put two predators in a pen and watch them tear themselves apart." Bloodlust lit up his eyes.

183

"The world will burn," I muttered, recalling the words of Dr Dabish.

"Yes, Dr Watson. The world... will... burn... And when it does, when government is gone and all that is left is ash, we will rebuild a new empire under my flagship."

"That was your game?" said Holmes. "You intend to play each country off the other and side with the one that wins."

"Check and mate, Mr Holmes."

Perny then fired his gun; Holmes fell to the floor. Azael jumped up laughing, acting like a crazed beast. Doctor Perny fired another shot in my direction. I dodged, withdrawing my revolver and returning fire. Perny evaded my bullet. I was then jarred by a flaming log which flew through the air towards Perny, striking him. I turned to find Holmes dropping a pair of tongs to dispose of Azael with a quick bartitsu move. I turned back to see that Perny had vanished from the room and the log was smouldering on the floor.

"Holmes, are you all right?" I cried.

"I am fine, fret not," said he. "We can't let Perny get away!" We ran from the room in pursuit. "Don't move! Be silent!" uttered Holmes when we reached the entryway.

Suddenly, I was ambushed from behind. Azael had woken and leapt on top of me. I fought to keep his hands from my neck, while Holmes grabbed him from behind. Azael screamed as Holmes dug into one of the man's pressure points. He let go and Holmes pushed him to the door. Azael lunged at Holmes, who then tossed him over his back and slammed him to the floor, cracking his head on the stone surface. I could smell smoke and looked back into the study, noticing the log which Holmes had tossed had caught fire to the rug and was quickly spreading to the furniture and walls.

"We need to get out of here, Holmes," I shouted.

"Not without Perny," he insisted.

"This place is going to burn!"

"And this man is mad enough to let the world burn just because he has the power to orchestrate it. Watson, even Moriarty had more sense. Perny is truly a new breed of the criminally insane."

We heard a door slam upstairs, and Holmes darted up the steps; I followed behind. I held my revolver ready, anticipating a sudden attack. When we reached the second floor, we slowly began checking each room. When I looked into one of the rooms, someone grabbed my arm and pulled me inside. I heard the door slam and Holmes pounding on it frantically. A figure in a respirator, similar to the one Dabish had worn, stood before me holding a unique gun connected by a hose to a pack strapped to the figure's back.

"It's time for you to die," said the figure.

The voice belonged to Perny. He pulled the trigger and released toxic fumes from inside the pack. I knew I didn't have long before the gas took over, and I became a victim of its horrible effects. I held my breath and shot out the window, hoping a draft of fresh air could buy me time. Perny rushed me, and I lost hold of the gun. I managed to kick him off, and I ran for the window. Standing on the ledge, I lowered myself as low as I could before dropping to the ground. When I landed, I twisted my ankle and was unable to stand. As I crawled a good distance from the burning mansion, I could still hear Doctor Perny laughing and Holmes calling my name. I felt dizzy from the gas and hearing gunshots from inside the house, worried for

Holmes's life. My head throbbed, and I felt myself starting to lose consciousness. As I drifted, the last thing I saw was a figure approaching me in the respirator. This was the end for me.

*****

I woke, and to my relief, I saw Sherlock Holmes standing over me. We were still outside the mansion, and I was lying in the grass. The house was lit up in a glorious blaze, and next to me lay the respirator mask.

"What happened in there?" I asked.

"He tried to kill me, and he failed," Holmes replied softly. "Watson, I was prepared to give my life if it meant stopping him. He released a strong dose of gas in the hallway and came at me. I held my breath as long as I could while we struggled. Then, he pulled a gun and tried to shoot, but I was able to reverse the odds, shooting him instead. When he fell, I took his mask and left him there."

"Are you all right, my friend?" I asked.

"I am. Come, the sun is rising; let us get you back home."

*****

We returned to Baker Street, where Mrs Hudson was fast at work cleaning up the mess from the explosion. She let out a screech when she saw Holmes and me in the condition we were in.

"Oh my! Mr Holmes, Doctor Watson, are you both all right?" she asked.

"I'm fine, woman," returned Holmes.

"We'd love some tea and perhaps some breakfast," I countered.

"Right away," replied Mrs Hudson as she left. Holmes sat in his usual chair, which didn't seem too damaged from the day before, and I, too, settled into my chair. We enjoyed the silence for some time. Even when Mrs Hudson brought us food and drink, not a word was spoken. In quiet, we nourished ourselves simply by being thankful to be alive.

Later that day, Inspector Lestrade strode into the study. By the look upon his face, he seemed glad to see us alive and well, yet an overwhelming sense of stress hung about him, no doubt caused by the events of the day before.

"Holmes! You both look like hell."

"Ah, you have never bid us such a splendid compliment before, Inspector," Holmes replied with a grin.

"So, are you going to tell me what in the world happened last night? You left me with quite the mess!" he said.

"Please, sit down, I'll tell you all," Holmes proceeded to do just that. He left out not the slightest detail. "However, Inspector," Holmes concluded, "I do not think the public would be able to cope with a resurrected evil Dr Perny, so I am perfectly happy with whatever you wish to print in the papers."

"We can deal with the papers later, Holmes. I'll need your services while this whole matter is put to rest."

I saw little of Holmes over the next month as he reassembled his evidence from all four cases and aided Lestrade in the recovery of Doctor Perny's body. They also located the remaining stores of Perny's deadly gas and destroyed every trace. The papers didn't reveal anything regarding Perny's involvement, but they did mention Admiral Hague and the discovery of a private mistress who had been held against her will, and acquired from the white slave trader, Laurent. There was very little mention of Holmes's involvement except for a few quick sentences that merely mentioned his consulting, but this didn't seem to bother him the few times I did see him. Over this period, we had work done to restore our lodgings at Baker Street, and when it was completed, it was quite marvellous. Though it did not take Holmes long to revert to his messy 'system', which cluttered our rooms with hordes of papers, books, and experimental equipment. Yet, though it was a mess, everything to him was in its proper place. He, and only he, knew the formula.

*****

As we sat together after breakfast one morning, Holmes noticed that I had been compiling all the data from the last four months of cases in my red journal.

"My dear Watson," said Holmes, holding his cherrywood pipe in his hand. "I wish that you would not yet publish these accounts. They are unique and wholly remarkable unto themselves. Never have I had a string of cases intrinsically connected, yet so grotesque that even I prefer not to be reminded of them so soon."

"As you wish, Holmes, I wouldn't want to put anything to paper that you do not prefer the public to see. Consider them locked away."

"You are a fine companion, old boy. Now, hand me that stack of letters. This clean-up has left me starved for a new case!" He inhaled deeply from his pipe as I handed him the morning mail. "Ah, here we are. A Mr James Phillimore was last seen stepping into his house to get his umbrella and has not been seen since. Most peculiar. Come, Watson," Holmes said enthusiastically, his eyes burning bright with the excitement and promise of further adventure, "the game is on! Let us be off at once!"

I put down my papers, took my coat and hat, and followed Sherlock Holmes out the door.

The End

The Strange Case of Mr Benjamin Goodwin

I recall one of the most horrific cases that has passed the threshold of 221b Baker Street. It was in the Autumn of 18– when a Mr Benjamin Goodwin was shown into our study.

"Mr Holmes?" asked the man, passing through the door.

"Ah, right on time. Come in, Mr Goodwin, and please take a seat! If you do not mind, my colleague, Dr Watson, will be joining me," Holmes said, extending his hand towards the sofa.

"Thank you for seeing me, Mr Holmes. And I do not mind Dr Watson sitting in, only if he has the stomach to handle my case. I am at my wits' end, and I need your assistance!"

"I have seen my fair share of unique cases. I should be able to handle your affair," said I.

"Very well," Mr Goodwin muttered.

"If you do not mind, I shall light my pipe." This was more of a statement than a question, as Holmes was already reaching for his Persian slipper.

"No, I do not. Carry on."

"Well, Mr Goodwin, your note sounded quite urgent. As you said, 'hell is at my doorstep.' Tell me how I can be of service," Holmes pressed, igniting his pipe.

"Mr Holmes, I, like you, am a man of reason, a man of science. I am a respected mathematics teacher at St Johns Boarding School here in the city and have a handsome home off Belgravia Mews. I do not entertain the idea of spiritual matters, as you read about these days! Ghosts lurking in graveyards, and what nonsense!"

"But something has rattled your beliefs?" I asked.

"Indeed, Dr Watson, it has. My eyes see one thing that my mind tells me is impossible. The simple calculation does not add up, and the problem remains that I know what I saw, and it is unexplainable by natural causes!" From the expression on Mr Goodwin's face, his eyes wide and his breathing heavy, I could see he was clearly troubled.

"I'm afraid that I am not the one to consult regarding any matters of spirituality. I am no foe to powers or beings beyond the physical realm," Holmes said dryly.

"Holmes, come now. Let us hear what the man has to say so that his trip is not a waste. Besides, you do not have much on your plate at the moment, if I remember correctly." Holmes looked at me, slightly agitated. He was never keen on folks gracing our door when all they had to offer were cases of supernatural quality.

"Correct you are, Watson. Very well, Mr Goodwin, tell us your tale." Holmes leaned back in his chair, crossed his legs, and listened.

"As I said, I am a very logical man. I can also say that my dear wife, Svetlanna, is a strong, logical woman. But I assure you, we are the victims of a terrible haunting. It started three weeks ago today, while I sat in my study on that windy evening. I was sorting through papers when I heard my wife call down for a pot of tea. I went downstairs, took the tray from the maid, and began walking upstairs to my wife's chamber. On my way, I received a frightful shock. When I looked out of the window, I saw, across the street, a woman wearing a mourning dress and staring right at me! I stood still for some time. Long enough, in fact, for my wife to be looking for me. She found me on the stairs and asked if everything was all right.

'That woman, under the street lamp, who is she? The sight of her frightened me,' I asked.

'What devilry. It can't be!' my wife whispered. She appeared more shocked than I.

'Do you know this woman?' I asked.

'No, I don't, how could I? Why don't you go see who she is. Run her off or fetch a policeman!' she cried.

'Very well.' I rushed down the stairs and opened the front door, but the mourner was gone. Completely vanished. I told my wife and ordered her to forget the event."

"Mr Goodwin," Holmes interrupted, "am I meant to believe that you were merely frightened by some woman standing outside your house at night? I hardly have time for such trifles."

"I admit that seeing something like that, at night, would indeed tap a nerve, Holmes," I defended our prospective client.

"Mr Holmes! That was only the beginning! Throughout the next week, my wife began to act strangely. Every little thing frightened her, and she hated to be left alone. At some inconvenience, I let her go with me on my daily errands, but after several days, it became too much. Being out in public became traumatic for her. She constantly looked over her shoulder as if expecting to be followed. Whenever I asked her about it, she gave no reply, just held on to me tightly. Soon, she confined herself entirely to her rooms, but any noise throughout the house still made her panic. I also noticed a particular paranoia whenever the post was delivered. The following Wednesday, just one week after the first incident, I was in my study writing a letter to my brother. It must have been around ten o'clock when I heard my wife scream horribly. When I looked up, I nearly fell out of my chair as I saw the same woman in a mourning dress standing under the streetlamp! I threw my pen down and stormed outside to confront this troubled person, but as I jerked the front door open, she let out a terrible screech and was engulfed in a plume of smoke. When the smoke cleared, she had disappeared." Mr Goodwin's tone was firm, and he was clearly shaken by these events.

"It seems like someone is playing a cruel joke on you, Mr Goodwin. Have you offended anyone recently?" I asked.

"I dare say not, Dr Watson. I am in good standing with all of whom I associate. But this is no prank! It's the work of the devil. You see, by the following week, my wife had become so distraught that she was confined to bed, burning with fever. Just last week, as I sat in the lounge reading, I saw the woman again! I walked to the front window to get a better look. She removed the black veil covering her face, and the horror I saw, it shall never escape my mind! A mutilated face, this surely was a daemon straight from the mouth of hell! It pointed at me and cried one word: 'Thief!' Then vanished into smoke, just as before!"

"I must say, Mr Goodwin, this is all rather engaging," Holmes mused. "So, in summation, for three weeks you have been tormented by what you believe to be a demonic being, resulting in the serious deterioration of your wife's health. Seeing that today is a Wednesday, you wish for me to accompany you tonight when the next visitation is due."

"That is exactly right, Mr Holmes! I know you fancy the complex and strange, and that is what I offer you here and now!"

"Indeed, you have. I shall accept the case, Mr Goodwin. Give us your address, and you can expect Watson and me to arrive at your house at precisely nine o'clock tonight, as all these events appear to take place around ten o'clock."

"I am very grateful for this, Mr Holmes! Very grateful, indeed! You can find us on the corner of Halkin Street and Belgravia Mews, house number 10. I trust tonight will be a light that illuminates the darkness we have suffered. I shall see you both this evening. Afternoon, Mr Holmes, Dr Watson." Mr Goodwin then rose and left us.

"Take care," said I, closing the door behind him. "What a spectacular tale, Holmes, but are you really going to challenge these powers of darkness that Mr Goodwin so earnestly believes are tormenting him?"

"It is a rather fantastic story, Watson. There are curious elements that I believe need investigating. Besides, as you said, I don't have much on at the moment, and I am in need of a little stimulation."

"And I'd rather you stimulate yourself with a fanciful tale than through your other means."

"Fret not, my dear Watson, I shan't be needing that at present."

Belgravia Mews

A little past nine, Holmes and I jumped into a hansom and made our way to Belgravia Mews. It was cool enough to see our breath as Holmes thanked and paid the driver.

"What a bloody cold night. I hope Mr Goodwin has a fire lit!" I chattered and rubbed my hands together. Holmes proceeded to walk away from Mr Goodwin's home. He approached the street lamp and looked down at the ground.

"Fire? Watson, who needs a fire when you have the mental stimulation of a promising case? That alone helps boil the blood on a night like this!"

"What are you doing, Holmes? The house is this way," I pressed.

"I'm making an observation, Watson." Holmes walked back towards me and darted up the steps to knock on the front door. We were greeted by a young maid.

"Good evening, gentlemen. Mr Goodwin is waiting for you in the parlour," she greeted us as we stepped into the lavishly decorated home. We followed her into the room where Mr Goodwin was seated.

"Ah, so very good to see you, Mr Holmes and Dr Watson," he said. "Sally, would you fetch us a fresh pot of tea?"

"Yes, sir," she replied, and left the room.

"You have a lovely home, Mr Goodwin," I mentioned, taking a seat.

"Thank you, Dr Watson. It suits us well," he returned.

"Mr Goodwin, might you show me to the lounge from where you last saw this mysterious mourning woman?" Holmes asked.

"Yes, right this way." We followed him out of the room and into the lounge. "It was in here, Mr Holmes. I sat in this chair and faced the window there. I saw the thing out under the street lamp." As Holmes looked around the room, the maid entered holding a tray.

"Your tea is ready, gentlemen," she said, setting it down.

"Thank you, Sally. That will be all," returned Mr Goodwin. "Here, Dr Watson, have a cup."

"Thank you kindly," I accepted the steaming cup of tea.

"Mr Holmes, would you care for one?" he asked.

"No, thank you. If you don't mind, would you take me upstairs to the spot where you first saw this woman?" he asked urgently.

"Yes, of course. If you will both follow me." We proceeded out of the room and up the stairs. "I was here on these steps, taking some tea to Svetlanna, when I saw the woman standing just out there by the lamp post," said Mr Goodwin, pausing halfway up the staircase.

"Very well. Now, I shall need to see your wife."

"Mr Holmes, I must protest. She's in a very poor state. The doctor ordered that her visitors be restricted to the maid and me only."

"Well, Mr Goodwin, if you would rather her be tormented to death than use my services, I should care not. Come, Watson, let us be off," returned Holmes.

"Holmes, really!" I cried.

"I speak only the truth. I should not want to waste my time or Mr Goodwin's. I cannot complete a thorough investigation without seeing his wife."

"You can be most unorthodox, Mr Holmes, though that should not come as a surprise. I do not wish to hinder your investigation. Come this way and I'll take you to Svetlanna,"

Mr Goodwin said, defeatedly. He walked to a closed door and gently opened it. We could hear the panicked voice of a frail woman inside.

"Who's there!? Benjamin, is that you?" she cried.

"Don't worry, my love, it is I. How are you feeling?" Mr Goodwin asked his wife.

"Like the devil himself is lurking in every corner. My head and stomach are in endless anguish, like I'm being devoured from the inside out! I can't bear this weight! I cannot do it!"

"Svetlanna, calm yourself. All is well and will be well. I've brought some very special people over to help us: Mr Sherlock Holmes and Dr John Watson. Do you mind if they come in and sit with you?"

"No, no, I don't mind, but you must stay with me. Don't… don't leave me alone," she said as she passed into a deep sleep.

"She's overworked herself," I said to Holmes.

"I won't leave you. There, there. Sleep now, my dear," Mr Goodwin soothed. "Mr Holmes, Dr Watson, you may come in quietly." I pushed the door open and we entered the room. Holmes walked over to Mrs Goodwin and rubbed her hand. Her eyes began to gently reopen and she looked at the three of us.

"Hello, Mrs Goodwin. I am Sherlock Holmes and this is Dr John Watson. We hope to clear this devilish matter up for you," said he in a soft voice.

"I hope that you can, my soul cannot bear this torment," she was suddenly interrupted by a coughing fit. "Ben! What is that creature outside the door!?" she cried, and we all turned.

"There is nothing there, my dear. Just calm down and breathe," her husband assured.

"The devil! The devil!" cried Mrs Goodwin, who then passed out cold. I took her pulse to check her vitals.

"She'll be out some time," said I.

"Your wife, Mr Goodwin, is most certainly in a bad state. What do you make of her condition, Watson?" Holmes asked.

"She appears to be suffering from delusions, caused by her ongoing illness. I would suggest it's a form of shock. I recall many a soldier in Afghanistan had similar symptoms. She mentioned her stomach was in pain. Do you mind if I examine her?" I asked.

"Our doctor has been most thorough. He has found nothing. What can you find?" Mr Goodwin said sternly.

"He might find the reason for your wife's illness!" returned Holmes. Mr Goodwin dropped his shoulders and hung his head.

"No, carry on, Dr Watson," said Mr Goodwin. Holmes and Mr Goodwin left me while I took a brief examination of the woman's abdomen. When I concluded, I called the two back in.

"Yes, there's severe cramping, which could explain the pain. I don't detect a fever, though. If she had one, it has passed. Has your wife lost a great deal of weight?"

"She has not!" Mr Goodwin replied strangely. "She's never been a hefty woman. Why?"

"I noticed some stretch marks on her. Still, I would believe this to be a result of severe shock and high levels of stress."

"Dr Watson! Of course, she's in shock! I told you it was this woman we saw! She has poisoned my beautiful

Svetlanna to keep her from regaining her health. But I assure you, she is not delusional!" roared Mr Goodwin angrily.

"Tea?" asked Holmes.

"Pardon me?" returned Mr Goodwin.

"If it's not too much trouble, I would like some tea now. I'm a bit chilly, and a warm cup of tea would do the trick."

"Just a moment," said Mr Goodwin as he turned and left the room, slightly confused.

"Holmes, that was hardly professional!" I scolded.

"I am in a profession all of my own, Watson. There are no set rules. Now, if you keep an eye out for Mr Goodwin." Holmes reached for a painting that hung directly above the bed's headboard. I watched the hall, and whilst I did so, Mrs Goodwin began to talk in her sleep.

"Wash the blood… can't get it off!" she murmured.

"Ah, here we are!" said Holmes. Behind the panelling was a hidden compartment in the wall. Holmes was digging inside, looking for unknown items.

"What have you found?" I asked.

"It appears to be letters, addressed to Mrs Goodwin. I shouldn't think it too much of a stretch that Mr Goodwin is in the dark on their existence," said Holmes.

"How did you know they were there?" I asked.

"The frame is tilted, and I noticed a slight scratch in the wall from where it had been often moved, clearly from someone lifting it and hiding something behind," he returned. We then heard Mr Goodwin returning.

"Here you are, Mr Holmes. I didn't ask if you took sugar, but I put a small spoonful in," said Mr Goodwin, walking through the door.

"Let us leave Mrs Goodwin in peace. I think I've learnt all I needed to learn from here," said Holmes.

"We can retire to the study. I asked the maid to light us a fire," Mr Goodwin said. We journeyed into the study where we were offered seats, which we accepted. Holmes took the cup of tea and had a small sip.

"Mind the time; it's already quarter to ten. If this mourning woman turns up, it should be soon," I warned.

"Indeed, Watson. I just have a few questions for you, Mr Goodwin," Holmes began.

"I'm listening, Mr Holmes."

"Tell us a little background about you and your wife, Svetlanna. She's from Russia, I gather, presumably where you met her and asked her to marry you, straight away taking her from her native land."

"My, Mr Holmes! You seem to know our history already!" he cried.

"A simple matter of deduction; passing through the house, I noticed there were no indications of her Russian heritage, all British. Though her accent was very strong; it indicates to me that she spent the majority of her life in Russia, only to quickly abandon it, likely for you, Mr Goodwin, a wealthy Englishman."

"Well, that is correct, Mr Holmes. I met Svetlanna fourteen years ago on a tour of Europe. She was alone and without family, and it broke my heart to see such a beautiful young woman in such a bad way. Well, my heart went out to her and we fell in love immediately. We wed, and she travelled with me back to England where we have been happily settled ever since," Mr Goodwin informed us.

"Do you have any children?" Holmes asked.

"Unfortunately not, Mr Holmes, that is something that stings my heart. When we returned to England, I wished to have a child as soon as possible, but she has not been of the same mind. She says children frighten her, and she wants to enjoy 'our time', as it were," he said.

"That is interesting…" but before I could finish, we were shockingly interrupted by a reverberating scream, which could have shattered glass, coming from Mrs Goodwin's room.

"Good Lord! What curse has fallen upon us!" cried Mr Goodwin.

"Quick, to your wife's room!" roared Holmes, and the three of us raced upstairs. We could hear Mrs Goodwin yelling in her room as we raced towards her.

"Stay back, you devil! Stay back!" We burst in the door and Mr Goodwin recoiled.

"What is that!?" he cried. And there, hovering in the bedroom window, was the figure of a woman dressed in a black mourning gown! Her face could not be seen as her body crashed into the window several times. Mrs Goodwin, by this time, had buried her face into her pillows and was moaning and weeping.

"Holmes, are you seeing this?! There's a flying… being!" I stammered, finding it hard to believe what my eyes were seeing.

"I see it, Watson," said Holmes rather coolly. Then, with a great whoosh, the figure vanished from sight. Holmes raced over to the window to look out. Mr Goodwin was over by his wife, stroking her hair and praying,

"Heavenly Father, please end this horrible curse! What great sin have I committed to deserve this?" Mr Goodwin mumbled tearfully.

"Watson, you and I shall go up to the roof! Is there a ladder, Mr Goodwin?" asked Holmes.

"There's a stair between this house and the next. At the top there's a ladder. The flat roof is a bit unstable, so do be careful," remarked Mr Goodwin.

"Watson, there's no time, let's go. Mr Goodwin, stay here and calm your wife; this has been quite the fright," ordered Holmes while we darted out.

*****

"What do you expect to find up here, Holmes, a creature that is flying about in the sky?" I asked as we climbed the ladder.

"Don't give in so easily to what your eyes see, Watson," Holmes replied.

"You must entertain the notion of another worldly presence. Men and women just don't fly away, Holmes!" said I as Holmes helped me over the ledge and we stood examining the rooftop.

"You are correct. But as I have said in the past, 'When you eliminate the impossible, whatever remains, however improbable, must be the truth'!"

"A clever line, yes. However, the truth is the impossible was just shown to be possible!" I protested.

"Or rather, the impossible was made to look possible," returned Holmes. He darted around the roof looking for clues, but all I could see was a small puddle where the roof was starting to sag. Holmes, looking over the edge, let out a cry. "These two screws here, we are directly above Mrs Goodwin's room; and see here, directly across from us is the ladder which we came up. In the centre of the roof is a puddle of water, which you just passed through walking towards me, Watson. You can clearly see where something was dragged through the puddle and went in this direction, then returned toward the staircase, which we came up. Something was hoisted down and kept in place by these screws," he pointed. "When the intended reaction was made, the item lowered was pulled back up, implying that it flew, then it was quickly taken away before we could get up here."

"Truly remarkable, Holmes, I missed that entirely!"

"And something else confirms my suspicions. Out on the pavement under the streetlamp, when you asked what I was doing, I observed two burn marks. I've seen similar markings like this in the past. Mr Goodwin said that the creature vanished in a puff of smoke. This makes me very certain of how this was done. Clearly, this 'being' used an exploding capsule which burst into a cloud of smoke on impact to mask its escape. It's an old Chinese trick," said he.

"Ah, like magicians use in their shows. But why would someone be doing this? I don't understand the motive. Mr Goodwin said there is no resentment amongst his associations."

"No, you are correct; Mr Goodwin has not upset anyone. I'm working on a theory at present, but it will take some time. Come, Watson, let us go back and speak with our host." Holmes and I returned to the house and were greeted by Mr Goodwin, who was still unnerved.

"What have you found, Mr Holmes?" he asked.

"I do believe that you are being tormented by an unknown being," said Holmes.

"This much I knew, Mr Holmes. I am not comforted by this whatsoever!"

"I did not intend to comfort you; however, it is clear that your tormentor is not otherworldly, as you suspect."

"Then pray tell! Who could it be?"

"That is out of my grasp still."

"Mr Holmes! I came to you to get answers, not to play childish games. If you cannot tell me who or what is threatening me, then I shall dispense with your services and seek assistance elsewhere. I must insist that you both leave!"

"Mr Goodwin, do calm down. It's been a very stressful night. Holmes found compelling evidence," I said, attempting to cool his mood.

"Never mind it, Watson. Mr Goodwin, I can promise you that by this time next week, all can be cleared up. If you wish for me to clear this matter up, you know where to find me." Holmes then turned and walked out the door.

I followed quickly behind and caught him as he was jumping into a hansom, which he ordered to go straight to Baker Street.

"Why did you just leave, Holmes? You didn't even tell him what we found on the roof, or of the burn marks!"

"The events of the night were too much for him to handle, Watson. He has built it up in his mind that this is a demonic attack; until he can see the light of reason, I can be of no assistance to him. However, I expect to hear from him within the next few days, but for now, I wish to get back to Baker Street!" and he spoke no more until we reached 221b.

Letters

We sat in the study, keeping warm by the fire. I asked Holmes if he'd care for a glass of brandy. "No, thank you. I have to give my full attention to the case."

"I thought you were leaving it till Mr Goodwin contacted you?" I asked.

"No, Watson. Remember these?" Holmes pulled out a bundle of letters.

"Ah, the letters you found in Mrs Goodwin's room. I had forgotten."

"We were interrupted before I could mention them to Mr Goodwin, and, given his state of mind at the end, I thought it best to look them over here." He opened them and began reading through them. "These are very interesting. Here, read this aloud." I took the letters into my hand and looked at them in confusion.

"Holmes, they are in Russian. You know I do not speak Russian."

"Oh yes. It is high time you made an effort to familiarise yourself with more languages, Watson. Fine then, I shall read it out. This one translates, 'Bad mother. Your sin is deep, and you will burn for your deed.' Another reads, 'The mourner will come.' The last one is, 'The mourner is here'."

"Ah, and from Mr Goodwin's testimony, it seemed as if his wife, Svetlanna, was expecting the mourning woman when she saw her."

"And when she finally arrived, Mrs Goodwin was so distraught that she made herself ill," finished Holmes.

"But why?" I asked.

"She bears a dark secret from her past, Watson. And it will soon be revealed. If you don't mind, I'd like to be alone with my thoughts," said Holmes.

"As you wish. I will return to this affair in the morning. Good night."

"Good night, Watson."

*****

It had been several days since our trip to Belgravia Mews, and not much had transpired. Mrs Hudson walked in and handed Holmes some letters, which he quickly skimmed over. "Look here, Watson! Here is a letter from Mr Goodwin. What did I tell you? He's had a change of heart. Let us hope these past three days have helped him clear his mind." He ripped open the note and read it quickly.

"What's in the note?" I asked.

"It seems that Mr Goodwin has been taken ill and he wishes to see us at our earliest convenience," said Holmes.

"Is it serious?"

"There is no indication either way. Well, let us be off at once then." We quickly made ourselves ready and took a hansom straight to Belgravia Mews, where we were greeted again by maid Sally, who took us into the parlour, where Mr Goodwin sat. His face was pale and thin, and he seemed somewhat dehydrated.

"Please, Mr Holmes, Dr Watson, come in and take a seat," he said in a weak and slurred tone.

"How are you feeling?" I asked.

"Not well. Whatever devilish curse has befallen my wife has now fallen on to me."

"Mr Goodwin, when did you first begin to feel ill?" asked Holmes.

"It was the evening after our encounter with the mourning woman, Mr Holmes," said he.

"Watson, what do you make of his condition?" Holmes pressed.

"Mr Goodwin, do you mind if I examine you?" I asked.

"Proceed, Doctor," he returned.

"There's evident slurred speech. You have a temperature, too. Have you eaten?"

"No, well, yes. I don't mind. A little bit."

"You don't mind what? Mr Goodwin?"

"I'm sorry, Dr Watson. My head is a little fuzzy."

"What have you eaten, Mr Goodwin?" I asked again.

"I had some fruit, a bit of bread. What does it matter? I've called you here for another reason. Mr Holmes, you said that this matter could be cleared up by Wednesday. Since your departure, I've called in a priest and a few other religious leaders, and nothing they have done has changed the state of this house. You tell me, what can you do?"

"I can ensure that, come Wednesday night, I will capture this spectre. Much like Abraham Van Helsing, I shall trap it and turn it to dust!" exclaimed Holmes.

"Then, please, do so! All my hopes rest on you, Mr Holmes." Mr Goodwin was now very weak and drifting into sleep.

"Holmes, Mr Goodwin needs to rest. I think we should leave him. I'll prescribe a diet to leave with the maid and make sure she knows to stick to it," I informed him.

"Yes, I agree, Watson. Mr Goodwin, we must leave you now for preparation. I shall call back on Wednesday when all will be set right."

"Thank you, Mr Holmes. My life… is in your hands…" said he as he dozed off. Holmes and I prepared to leave, but not before speaking to maid Sally.

"Miss Sally?" I called.

"Yes, Doctor?" she returned.

"We have a few questions for you," said Holmes.

"Go on," she replied nervously.

"Don't worry. You are in no trouble," Holmes comforted. "I am wondering though, on Thursday, did you go out at all, perhaps to the market?"

"As a matter of fact, I did. I went to Covent Garden and purchased some fresh fruit and vegetables for the house," she informed us.

"Did anything unique happen?" I asked.

"Oh Lord, it's my fault, isn't it?!" she cried.

"What happened?" Holmes asked.

"Well, Mr Goodwin likes grapefruit, and well, I purchased one for him, and on my way out of the market, I tripped over someone's foot and fell into this woman. Some of our groceries fell on the floor, and it's possible that our grapefruits were swapped, as she had one too," finished the maid.

"Yes, I should think that was no accident. Mr Goodwin was expected to eat it. But whoever this person was did not intend to kill him, or they would have used a stronger poison," said Holmes.

"Oh, dear! Oh dear! I was such a fool!" she said.

"Come now, my dear. What's done is done. You had no idea what was happening. If anything, Mr Goodwin was the fool for wishing us away the other night," assured Holmes.

"I do hope you can clear up this matter, Mr Holmes," she pleaded.

"Wednesday, all will be clear, though do me a favour. On Wednesday, keep the windows open on the second floor, and when Mr Goodwin is feeling better, instruct him to stay inside and not leave the house until we return next week."

"As you wish, Mr Holmes, I'll tell him," she replied.

"Very good. There is nothing more we can do until Wednesday. Until then, Miss," said Holmes, and he and I left, but not before I gave instructions to her on Mr Goodwin's diet.

The Mourner Cometh

The rest of the week went by quickly, as we soon found ourselves preparing for another meeting with the mourning woman. I sat in a hansom while Holmes was speaking with one of his Irregulars. "Holmes! Come on, I cannot hold the cab much longer!" I cried, and he turned and ran over.

"Thank you, Watson. I was just giving Purdy some instructions. Now, cabbie, take us to 10 Belgravia Mews!" and the hansom pulled away.

"What was your instruction?" I asked.

"I have passed on a message to Lestrade to meet us tonight at eleven o'clock. By then the deed will be done," replied Holmes.

"How are you so sure?" I asked.

"Elementary. With each visit, the mourning woman has come closer and closer. It only makes sense that her next move will be to enter the house. When she does, we shall trap her!"

"Feels like a stretch, but I hope you're right."

"I am, Watson," Holmes promised. We arrived at Belgravia Mews and maid Sally showed us into the parlour where Mr Goodwin was. He was looking more nourished.

"Mr Holmes, it brings me great joy to see you," he said in a stronger tone.

"It is nice to see you are feeling better, Mr Goodwin," returned Holmes.

"Yes, whatever devilry was upon me seems to be passing," said he, nodding.

"Food poisoning, Mr Goodwin. That is the devilry," remarked Holmes.

"You have no evidence of that, Mr Holmes!" he shouted.

"It was but a week ago that you sat in my study and told me that you are a logical man. Now I am finding you highly illogical in your reasoning."

"And I see you are not afraid to keep a closed mind and continue insulting my intelligence. I have yet to receive proof that this is something other than a supernatural happening," he retorted.

"At the end of tonight, this will all be cleared up," Holmes said.

"As you wish, so tell me, Mr Holmes, how do you expect to capture this thing? I have a book here on enchantments; it might be of use."

"Oh, Mr Goodwin, do be serious! If you do not wise up, perhaps I shall draw a magic circle and tell you that if you pass through, you'll burn to death," Holmes scoffed.

"Holmes! What is the matter with you?" I asked.

"I'm sorry, I just do not have patience for this superstitious nonsense." Then, the clock chimed.

"It's quarter to ten," I acknowledged.

"Ah yes, we shall take positions!" Holmes said.

"What positions are these?" asked Mr Goodwin.

"I want you and Miss Sally to remain on the first floor. Go sit in the front room. Understood, Mr Goodwin?"

"Yes," he replied.

"Well, go on. There is no time like the present," ordered Holmes. "Watson, let us go up into Mrs Goodwin's bedroom; that is where we are needed."

"Very well," and I followed. When we reached the door, Holmes and I quietly entered.

"Hide on the other side of the bed, next to the vanity opposite the window. I'll be in the corner behind the large chair," whispered Holmes, not wanting to wake the sleeping woman.

"All right."

I have always trusted Holmes's judgement, but I admit that I was somewhat sceptical that this mysterious woman would turn up. As I sat there hiding behind the vanity, I heard a strange, haunting noise coming from outside the house. I kept my eyes fixed on the window. Then, I saw her. The woman in a mourning dress slipping in the window! My heart raced as she lowered herself into the room. I waited for Holmes to make a move, but he didn't. The woman walked up to the bed where Mrs Goodwin lay resting and ran her pale hand along the side of the bed.

Then, she spoke in Russian, which I was able to have translated by Holmes: "So finally, we come face to face. You, who treated me like an animal, who tossed me out like a bag of garbage. You, who left for money and wealth. You disgust me. The hell I put you through compares little to the hell I have endured. You superstitious fool," and the woman pulled out a large, sharp knife. "This is the only thing wealth can bring. Grief, pain, and death!" she hissed.

"Stop there!" cried Holmes, lunging and restraining the woman. Mrs Goodwin awoke and screamed in terror. Holmes struggled with the attacker, subduing her and tossing the knife to the side as Mr Goodwin rushed in.

"What is going on? Svetlanna, are you all right?" he cried.

"Demon… the demon!" Mrs Goodwin babbled.

"Let me go, you fool!" the would-be killer protested in rough English.

"Here, Mr Goodwin, is your demon! Watson, take off the veil." I did so, and we saw this mourner's face was indeed mutilated, scarred by some horrific event. It was also clear that the woman was young, about twenty years old.

"I don't understand, who is she?"

"She, Mr Goodwin, is the daughter of your wife!" announced Holmes.

"What?" Mr Goodwin said in shock.

"No! What have I done?" sobbed Mrs Goodwin.

"Mr Holmes, explain this now!" demanded Mr Goodwin.

"You were never haunted by a demon. When you first told me that this woman vanished in a plume of smoke, I assumed it was an old vanishing trick. On my first visit, I observed two burn marks on the ground where the capsules had exploded. Further, when the 'being' hung in the window last week, I discovered two hooks that had been screwed into the side of the house, conveniently above Mrs Goodwin's window. I also observed that something large had been dragged through a puddle of water, probably a dummy that could be lowered and quickly retrieved. This, Mr Goodwin, I would have said had you not coldly turned Dr Watson and me away," chided Holmes. "You said it yourself, Mr Goodwin, that when your wife saw this woman she acted as if she might have known who it was. The truth is she did. I found these letters behind the painting over the bed. They are threats that a 'mourning woman' would be coming. When the promised spectre arrived, it sent her into shock, to the point of illness for several weeks."

"How did you get those letters?" yelled Mrs Goodwin.

"Scratches on the wall from where the painting was frequently moved indicated something was hidden behind, and Mr Goodwin, your sudden illness was no demonic attack. No, the maid informed us that on her trip to the market, she had tripped. I deduced that the one thing that happened to be swapped when she collided with another woman was a grapefruit, which only you eat. It was clear that someone wanted you out of the way, and that someone was her, the mourning woman!

"But how can this woman be my wife's child?" asked Mr Goodwin, looking at the woman on the floor.

"Stretch marks, Mr Goodwin. When Watson examined her, he said he saw a fair amount of stretch marks on her stomach. Seeing that your wife is both very thin and does not bear any other stretch marks, it was a simple deduction that she had given birth. This is her daughter, come to seek revenge for being abandoned when she was but a small child, when her mother ran off with a rich Englishman," revealed Holmes.

"Svetlanna, is this true?" Mr Goodwin asked.

"Not a day has gone by that I haven't regretted what I did! I was young and immature. I thought if you knew you'd stop loving me," she wailed.

Mrs Goodwin's daughter roared something in Russian, which Holmes informed me was: "So you gave me up! All for the love of a man! You abandoned me in hell. See me now, my distorted face. The way I am is because of you! The family you left me with mutilated me! While you enjoyed your riches, I was left to be treated like a dog. You make me sick!"

"I'm sorry, if I could start over and fix everything, I would!" Mrs Goodwin returned in Russian. Then, there was a loud bang on the door, and we could hear the voice of

Inspector Lestrade demanding that someone let him in. Sally complied, and Lestrade rushed up the stairs.

"Halloa, halloa, halloa, what have we here?" he asked.

"Inspector, I have one mourning woman to hand over to you. On the charge of the attempted murder of Mrs Svetlana Goodwin, the poisoning of Mr Benjamin Goodwin, and harassment of the Goodwin household these past five weeks," said Holmes.

"Very well. Boys, take this woman away. I'm sure Mr Holmes is tired of holding her back," commanded Lestrade.

"Get off me! Let me go! She deserved it!" the mourning woman cried as she was dragged away.

"Thank you, Lestrade," returned Holmes.

"Now that this horror is over, Mr and Mrs Goodwin, I shall leave you both," said Holmes.

"As one horror ends, so another begins," sighed Mr Goodwin as he looked at his wife, who lay in bed with tears rolling down both their faces. "I am not sure if I am thankful, but nevertheless, we have answered." I looked at Holmes and motioned that we make our way, given that there was no more use we could be. With a gentle nod in reply, Holmes and I left the Goodwin family to deal with their horrific past.

SHERLOCK HOLMES & The Horror of Frankenstein

Introduction

In November 1987, during a renovation of 221B Baker Street, a secret compartment was discovered in the old wooden floor. Inside this compartment rested a thick folder inscribed with the name Dr John Watson. Within the folder were the pages of a never-before-seen case. Knowing the historic significance of these rooms, the papers were sent to the British Museum and their authenticity checked. Once the tests proved positive, the only known relative of Dr John Watson, who lives in London, was summoned, and the papers were read, in full, for the first time.

The first document was a letter from the famous doctor, and a remarkably horrific tale followed. The original papers have since been scanned and reprinted. This is the reprint.

The Letter

It is important to note that the events I have written down are entirely true. Disregard what the newspapers said, as they were given false reports. I know not who will be the first to read these papers, though I dare not share them for fear of my reputation and sanity being questioned. Sherlock Holmes and I have experienced a great number of tribulations and witnessed many horrific events, but none compare to this horror which fell upon us so swiftly. Take my word as gospel; sometimes myths and legends are indeed far more real than we are aware.

Dr John H. Watson
An Account Recorded by John H. Watson, M.D.

It was a cold and rainy October night in 18–. Between my marriage and medical practice, I had very little time to devote to rushing about London solving mysteries with my friend Sherlock Holmes. Though, as chance would have it, I found myself returning to those familiar rooms. My wife had recently been called away for a few weeks, and it opened the ideal opportunity to visit my friend. I sent Holmes a telegram informing him of Mary's departure, and he speedily replied, telling me to come and take up my old room while she was away. Before I knew it, I was standing outside 221B Baker Street. Mrs Hudson greeted me and informed me that Holmes was in the study, and that his mood was somewhat on the unpleasant side.

I found him slouched down in his chair in front of a popping fire. His hair was dishevelled, his eyes bloodshot, and his face looked painfully thin. Wrapped around his arm was a rubber band, and lying on the table next to him was a syringe.

"Holmes, you know how much I dislike the use of that substance!" I ejaculated in frustration, seeing him in such a dilapidated state.

"My dear Watson, that is hardly any way to greet a friend whom you have not seen for many a week," he returned.

"My apologies, old boy, I just do not care to see you this way," said I.

"Unfortunately, Watson, I have had nothing to engage my mind. London, it seems, has become utterly void of any interesting criminals."

"I hardly see that as a horrible thing, Holmes!"

"For you, yes. For me, the strange is what fuels my mind. Without the fuel, I must find a substitute."

"Come now, I can see a stack of letters here on the mantel. Are none of them of any interest?"

"Trifles! They are all trifles."

"Here, take this morning's paper." I handed him The Daily Telegraph. "There's been a string of grave robberies recently; is there no avenue to travel with that?" I asked.

"What crime is there in robbing graves? The people being robbed are dead and care not for their missing trinkets. The most I'd be doing is finding more inmates for Bedlam," sighed Holmes.

"It is the principle!" I exclaimed. "Leave the dead to rest, not pilfer their graves for little trinkets."

"Does not every archaeological expedition do such a thing, Watson? Digging around in ancient tombs, uncovering long-buried secrets, stealing old artefacts from the long dead, simply because no one remembers them, is no different from stealing artefacts from the recent dead. It's only frowned upon because their memory still lingers," Holmes finished.

I dared not continue the conversation with him. He had made up his mind on the issue and was not in the mood to change it. He began to scan The Daily Telegraph, making little grunts whenever he read something which amused him. Mrs Hudson knocked on the door and asked if we were ready for our evening meal. Holmes, who looked like he hadn't eaten in weeks, did not give her an answer, but I turned and told her that we would eat.

"Holmes, your diet has worn you thin; you must eat," I encouraged.

"And marriage, it seems, has kept you full," Holmes remarked with a grin upon his face.

"Maybe you should try it sometime," said I.

"I couldn't think of anything more horrific than marriage. I'll leave that to you."

It was not long before Mrs Hudson brought us some beef slices and gravy, which we happily ate. The wind was howling outside, and little pellets of rain were splashing against the window. When we had just finished, and I had taken the last sip of my brandy, there was a knock on the door.

"Enter!" said Holmes rather dramatically.

In walked Inspector Bradstreet, dripping from the rain.

"Ah, Inspector, do come in. Would you care for a drink?"

"No, thank you. I need your immediate assistance, Mr Holmes," said Bradstreet with great urgency.

"What has occurred?" I asked.

"The watchman at Nunhead Cemetery was found brutally murdered, his neck strangled."

"And another grave has been robbed, has it not?" asked Holmes.

"It has. We believe whoever is behind the other grave robberies is behind this one."

"Most engaging," Holmes muttered.

"I thought you found it all very boring, Holmes?" I asked.

"That was before there was a murder, which means these robbers were desperate. Come, Watson! Get your coat and boots; we shall be off straight away to Nunhead, where it's bound to be wet and muddy."

*****

Holmes and I rode with Inspector Bradstreet to the old cemetery. I have never spent much time in graveyards, nor cared to do so at night. Scattered about were grave markers of various designs: tall statues of weeping angels, arched stones tilted and covered in moss, and large crypts holding several bodies apiece. As we entered the cemetery, I could see several officers standing near an open crypt, the light of swaying lanterns illuminating their cold, wet faces.

The three of us stepped out of the carriage. The rain had subsided, and a thick fog had started to roll in.

"Well, well, well, what do we have here?" Holmes asked, approaching the other officers.

"The body is here," one of them said.

Holmes took a lantern and knelt down to examine it.

"Come see, Watson," motioned Holmes, and I followed. The body was soaked from the rain, as the watchman had clearly been lying there for several hours. It was evident that the man's neck was broken, and we observed severe bruising. There was also a small gash on the man's forehead, which looked like the result of blunt force trauma.

"What do you make of it, Mr Holmes? To us, it looks like the watchman was chased down and then ambushed here, where something hit him over the head before strangling him to death," commented Bradstreet.

"By the look on the man's face, he seems… petrified!" said I.

"Yes, indeed, Watson," said Holmes. "However, Inspector, you have missed something. The watchman was never chased, and he was not hit over the head, then strangled. We can safely say he was simply strangled. Judging by these marks on his neck, whoever strangled him had large hands. It is clear, by the imprint of the bruising, that it was only one large hand which strangled the life out of him before throwing the body aside, where the head cracked open upon this tombstone," Holmes pointed to the tombstone's chipped top. He also felt around on the ground and picked up the pieces of the broken stone. "You see, Inspector?" he finished.

"How can you tell this happened like that?" asked Inspector Bradstreet sceptically.

"It is simple. The man was most certainly never chased by the fact that it had been raining off and on all day. The ground here is very moist, and footprints are easily made. I can see where this man walked at a normal stride up to this point; that indicates he was not chased. He was walking when someone ambushed him. Whoever it was grabbed him and strangled him before throwing him. The watchman's head hit the tombstone, causing the gash on his forehead. Now, how do I know it happened in that order? The amount of blood on the head wound indicated that his heart had stopped beating beforehand. If the blood had been flowing, there would be much more of it to show. Besides, if someone was grabbed and tossed by another as large as this attacker, surely he'd run for safety. A hit to the head like this wouldn't immobilise him," finished Holmes.

"That's an interesting interpretation of the facts, Mr Holmes. I can see how you reached your conclusion. Are you sure we are only dealing with one person?" asked Bradstreet.

"Most certainly. Looking through the enormous number of footprints caused by your own men, there are indeed only two other prints: the watchman's and the grave robber's. I'd also say the person we are looking for is about eight feet tall, heavy, with large hands and feet."

"Explain your reasoning."

"We have their footprint," he replied, pointing to a puddle of water not far from the crypt. Bradstreet examined it more closely and realised Holmes was correct.

"By Jove! How did you see that?" cried Bradstreet, somewhat embarrassed to have missed it himself.

"I saw it because I was looking for it," said Holmes. "Tell me, what do we know of the body which was stolen?"

"Nothing, other than it was a young girl who was buried just yesterday," Bradstreet informed us.

"Yesterday, you say? That is interesting," remarked Holmes.

"So, we're looking for a giant man roaming graveyards at night. Surely he can't be too hard to find," I retorted.

"Indeed, we are. Let us return to Baker Street. I must gather more data before we can continue."

With that, Holmes and I were taken back to 221B, where he requested that he be left alone, and, given the late hour, I made my way to my room, retiring for the night.

*****

I awoke the next morning to find the weather had not improved. A thick fog was streaming through the street, making it nearly impossible to see people walking or driving carts as they tried navigating through it. I was at my toilet, preparing for the day, when I was startled by a loud yelp followed by Holmes shouting, "Magnificent!" I put on my robe and dashed down into the study, where I found him leaning on a table piled with articles and newspapers. His pipe was in his hand, and he had a suspicious grin on his face.

225

"What in blazes, old man! Is everything all right?" said I, bursting into the study.

"It is, old boy. I seem to have made a discovery. There is something unique about each grave robbery. Watson, you were following the stories in the papers; can you tell me what their unique qualities are?" he returned with a grin.

"Other than being morbidly grotesque, I cannot say."

"Women!" he exclaimed excitedly. "Each grave robbed belonged to a woman. Here, look at this," he pointed to the newspapers laid out on the table. "The grave robbed in Whitechapel was a woman, followed by a robbery in St Pancras Old Church, and then one in Tower Hamlets Cemetery. All of these graves belong to bodies which were rather old, five to ten years apart from the most recent two, Nunhead being the freshest."

"For what reason would these graves have been robbed, other than for buried riches?" I asked.

"That crossed my mind. According to the official reports, the only things stolen were the bodies, and everything else was left behind, even the clothes of the dead."

"Yes, of course! I recall that now. I found that quite disturbing. Stripping the bodies of the dead—a horrible thought." Holmes nodded in agreement. "So why are they taking the bodies and leaving the riches?"

"There is a pattern to these robberies, Watson. It seems I was mistaken to ignore the stories," he admitted.

"I did tell you, Holmes."

"Yes, but never mind that now. The pattern I have discovered is thus: with each robbery, the bodies taken have become fresher. The first few women were dead ten to five years, but the last two bodies were not in their graves any longer than a day or two," he paused, taking a puff of his pipe. "Not only that, but all the women came from noble lineage."

"What is the point of it all?"

"That is what we must find out."

"How so?"

"By a stroke of luck, a young woman named Isabelle Hawthorn is to be buried in West Ham Cemetery tomorrow. She is of noble lineage and comes from a wealthy family."

"That is hardly a stroke of luck! I do recall the name, though. She is the daughter of Lord Hawthorn. Tragic, really; the poor girl died of consumption, it seems."

"Nevertheless, Watson, she makes the ideal target. If these robbers are looking for women's bodies with the least decay and noble lineage, this is perfect. So you and I must stake out in the graveyard tomorrow night and hope that the body snatcher turns up! It's bound to be cold and wet, so remember to dress warmly."

*****

The next night, Holmes and I made our way to the graveyard. There was a soft drizzle and mild fog in the air, but nothing that proved to be of any obstruction to our efforts. We hid ourselves within West Ham Cemetery, keeping an unlit lantern nearby as we waited patiently for any activity. The late Miss Isabelle Hawthorn's grave was well within our sights. I could see that the dirt covering the freshly made grave was damp from the drizzle, and the flowers left behind by the mourners were tattered by the strong wind, which was ripping petals away.

I felt a chill run up my spine as we sat there waiting amid those solemn graves, though Holmes had nerves of steel and our location had no effect on him whatsoever. His hawk-like nose and grey eyes shifted this way and that as he looked out for any sign of interest. I heard the snap of a twig and quickly turned, my hand on my revolver, ready for action. Holmes let out a quiet laugh.

"This is hardly the time for a laugh!" said I in a stern whisper.

"Fret not, Watson. You jump at nothing. Merely a small stick falling from a tree."

"Holmes, we've been here for hours, and we've seen no activity whatsoever. Perhaps it's time we leave?"

"Steady, Watson. The night is far from over. Besides, we'll be able to handle whatever comes our way."

"It's not the grave robber that has me worried. I am simply not keen on spending nights in graveyards," I admitted.

"Superstitious nonsense, the dead will not be pouring from their graves tonight," said Holmes. Suddenly, my friend paused, his eyes widened, and he turned his head the other way. "Stay down, someone's coming!"

I looked over and saw someone walking through the yard. The figure, male, was tall and thin with wild hair. My heart began to race as he slowed down upon nearing the Hawthorn grave. To my relief, he carried on and was out of sight. I jolted when I heard an owl hoot.

"That is no bird, Watson."

"What is it then?"

"A signal," he replied.

Off in the distance, we could see another incredibly large figure lurking. He wore frayed clothes and was easily eight feet tall. Large hands hung low as the arms swung back and forth with every step of his gigantic feet. Whoever this was, he went straight to the grave of Miss Hawthorn and stood over it for several moments. Next, he dove to the ground and began to furiously dig. I could hear him groan as he ripped up the dirt and tossed it. I had never seen anyone dig with such force; it was almost inhuman—ape-like, perhaps. Holmes and I simply watched in disbelief as he tore into the ground. It took him little time at all before we heard a thud and crack as he reached the coffin and tore it open.

"Come, Watson, now is the time!" shouted Holmes. With revolvers drawn, we charged the grave robber, who had tossed Miss Hawthorn's naked body onto the ground and was climbing out of the hole. "The game is up!" announced Holmes.

"Stop right there!" I ordered.

"Turn and show us your face," demanded Holmes.

Picking up the dead body by its arm, the man stood upright with his back to us. He towered over Holmes and me. The skin of his arms was sickly and nearly translucent. The muscles beneath were tense.

"Do as you're told!" I ordered again. The man began to chuckle, from deep within his chest, at our demands. He slowly turned and faced us. The moment he did, a bolt of lightning lit up the sky and revealed the man's—if a man he was—face. It was truly horrific, not that of a normal man. This was something demonic. It was the perfect picture of decay.

"What unholy union has been formed to create a creature such as this!" uttered Holmes as he gazed upon the foul features of this being. We took a few steps back. The creature only growled. Then, with immense speed and strength, he flung his long, bulky arms and struck Holmes and me, tossing us to the ground. I dropped my gun and could not see where it had fallen. I looked over and saw the creature pick up the dead woman and lumber towards Holmes, who seemed to have lost his firearm as well.

"Now would be an adequate time to shoot, Watson!" yelled Holmes.

I then saw the unlit lantern that we had brought. I reached into my coat, pulled out my lighter, and lit the lantern. I rushed upon the beast and shattered the lantern upon his back, causing the oil inside to ignite in flames as it splattered all over it. The daemon immediately lit up in flames, along with the body of Miss Hawthorn. Howling in pain, the creature dropped the woman's body and took off, awkwardly running into the night.

"I couldn't find my gun, that was the best I could do," I told Holmes, helping him to his feet.

"I'm glad you did it," he replied.

"Holmes, what was that thing?"

"A monster."

*****

I tossed and turned all night in my bed. The face of that monster had been ingrained in my mind. The way he effortlessly ripped up the earth and handled the dead woman's body before hurling both Holmes and me a fair distance with the strength of his gigantic arms—needless to say, sleep was not something that I could take comfort in upon returning to our lodgings. When I finally managed to slip into a dreamless sleep, I was suddenly thrust from my slumber with a loud knock on my door. Groggy, I sat up. The handle turned, and in popped Holmes.

"Get ready, we are leaving in five minutes."

"Where are we going!?" I cried.

"Chop, chop!"

"Very well," I grumbled exhaustedly. I quickly prepared myself and found Holmes waiting at the bottom of the stairs by the front door, his arms crossed and his foot tapping. "I'm ready, I'm ready."

We jumped into the third hansom. "Why did you drag me out of bed, Holmes? I barely had four hours of sleep."

"Well, then you've already had three hours more than I," said he. "I had a most productive night, which has led me to this new avenue. We are on our way to see a woman by the name of Miss Victoria Walton."

"Victoria Walton. I seem to recall the name. Was it not her grandfather who, after failing to become a writer, captained a ship that went to explore the North Pole?" I asked.

"She is, indeed, his granddaughter."

"What does she have to do with this, though?"

"More than the wider public knows." We soon found ourselves outside the front door of Miss Walton. It was one of many which lined the Georgian street. I knocked and waited for an answer. The door swung open, and before us stood a petite woman. She had rosy cheeks and lovely curly auburn hair. Her eyes were big and green, and her skin was almost golden. She was, indeed, a handsome woman.

"May I help you?" she asked.

"Are you Miss Walton?" Holmes replied.

"Indeed, I am," she returned.

"Then I believe you can help us. I am Sherlock Holmes and this is Doctor John Watson. We need to speak with you regarding a most sensitive topic which is connected to your grandfather, Captain Robert Walton."

"What is it about?" she asked nervously.

"Frankenstein's Monster," Holmes said in an eerie whisper.

Her eyes widened, and her face turned pale as she bit her lower lip. "I'm afraid I cannot help you, Mr Holmes," she returned and began to shut the door.

"And what if the creature is back?" Holmes asked softly. Miss Walton paused. Her hands were shaking, and her eyes were shifting.

"Come in," she said reluctantly, and opened the door for us to enter. As we passed through, I saw her scan the street for prying eyes. She closed the door, and we were taken into the lounge where we took a seat. "No one has mentioned the name of Frankenstein in decades."

"Miss Walton, what can you tell us about the Frankenstein monster?" Holmes asked. I sat soaking up the conversation. As I was unclear as to what the Frankenstein monster was, I finally asked,

"What is the Frankenstein monster?"

"It is nothing but a myth nowadays, Watson. However, I remember reading once that Miss Walton's grandfather possessed papers documenting a so-called monster attack in Geneva back in 1818, but he never disclosed them."

"You think I know where these papers are?" asked Miss Walton.

"Elementary, Miss Walton. You are the only direct descendant of Robert Walton. If the events were true and so terrifying, he'd keep the papers locked away and pass them on to his next of kin; that would be you.

"And you believe this monster is back?" she pressed.

"I do. I believe it is here in London. If I could see the papers, it would be most helpful," said Holmes.

"I don't have the papers, they are, as you guessed, locked away. No, no, do not worry, I know the story by heart," said Miss Walton.

"For heaven's sake! Monsters? Holmes, what is going on here?"

"Miss Walton is about to tell us."

"It happened in 1818. My grandfather was a young, ambitious man. When he failed to become a writer, he decided he'd try to increase his scientific knowledge and explore the Arctic. He thought this might bring him the fame he always wanted. While he was sailing the frozen waters, he stumbled upon a man on the verge of death. This man was Victor Frankenstein. Once they got him into the cabin and gave him food and warm clothes, he began to rant about his quest for a giant monster that he was chasing. Frankenstein told my grandfather that he was a scientist who had the idea to try to create life, not through conception, but through purely scientific means. He had stolen from graves and assembled body parts to create his creature. Frankenstein thirsted for the power of God. He used advanced sciences and succeeded in creating a horrible abomination. God himself turned his face away from this monster. When Frankenstein saw what he had created, he was mortified. He had no right to play God. That power was not his to wield.

"Overcome by the horror of his experiment, Frankenstein fled into the mountains and abandoned his creation, but the creature soon found his reclusive creator. The monster had, by this time, developed its cognitive abilities and pleaded for a chance to share its tale. It told of its own journey, and its realisation that it would never be accepted into society because of its hideous origins and brutish appearance. The creature begged Frankenstein to create for it a companion, a bride. Reluctantly, Victor agreed and came to England to build a companion for the creature. In the midst of creating the second creature, Frankenstein was burdened with worry, fearing what would happen if these two creatures spawned offspring. Tormented by this thought, coupled with the desire to go and be with his fiancée, Elizabeth, he destroyed the female creature and left.

"Frankenstein knew that his creation would surely come after him when it found out what he had done, so he rushed back to Geneva to marry his dear Elizabeth so that together they could flee and hide from the monster. However, the creature, which was close on their heels, found Elizabeth and strangled her to death to show its creator the pain it felt. Frankenstein, then realising that his creation was nothing but a killing machine, sought to destroy it; he followed the monster far up north, where my grandfather found him. All turned sour for Frankenstein when the creature found him inside my grandfather's ship and strangled him to death. It was then that my grandfather saw the monster for the first time and believed in the true horror of Frankenstein. He told us he thought that the creature was satisfied in the wake of its creator's death, so he let the creature go and watched it drift off into the distance where it would surely meet a frozen grave."

"My word, are you telling me that we are hunting a zombie?" I asked.

"No, Watson, not a zombie. We are hunting a mad scientific experiment," returned Holmes.

"Mr Holmes, I must be honest with you. You are not the first person in recent weeks to seek out information regarding this tale. Some time ago, I was approached by a vile man in hopes of sailing into the Arctic to find this frozen creature. He tried to get information from me regarding my grandfather's expedition but, repulsed by him, I did not aid. He was wicked with a crazed look in his eye!" exclaimed Miss Walton.

"What did this man look like?" asked Holmes.

"He was tall and thin with frizzy white hair, beady eyes, and a pointed nose," she informed.

"And did you not get a name?" I asked.

"I'm sorry, but I did not. As I said, he was most terrifying, and I wished to part with him without delay."

"Thank you, Miss Walton, you have been informative. If you will excuse us, we must be off now!" Holmes suddenly announced.

"Be careful, Mr Holmes! There was not a time when my grandfather wasn't looking over his shoulder, worried that one day the monster might return. 'Death is the creature's only path', he used to say." With that, Holmes and I bade Miss Walton adieu and left.

"What do you think that man wanted with the information from Miss Walton?" I asked Holmes as we walked along.

"I am not sure, however I do know that it is no coincidence that Miss Walton was questioned about Frankenstein's monster prior to these suspicious grave robberies. It seems frightfully clear what is going on," he replied with certainty.

"Which is?"

"Someone is constructing the monster's bride!"

"What sort of mad science are we dealing with!" Holmes merely looked at me. "So, you don't think we are after a real monster?" I asked.

"Any person who believes they can create life out of the dead is already monstrous, mark my words."

"What I still don't understand is what inclined you to go and see this Miss Walton."

"When we returned last night, I could not get that horrible beast out of my mind. It was then that I recalled an old German myth about a man-like monster who tormented a small village in Geneva, but of course, the witnesses were few, and it passed into folklore. I was, however, fortunate enough to have a catalogue of names associated with this event, the two most prominent being Frankenstein and Walton. Within my files, I had stored a newspaper clipping from the day Captain Walton died, talking about his connection to this folktale, and that, though he had apparent paper documentation regarding the events, he refused to share them publicly."

"Outstanding, Holmes! Your habitual storing of useless information has most certainly paid off!" I cried.

"It is not useless to retain a plethora of information which can be made readily available upon request. Now we must put an advertisement in the papers if we are to set a trap!" Holmes declared grandly while flagging a passing hansom, which we jumped inside.

*****

"Do you think this will work?" I asked as Holmes, and I stood in a dark, round operating chamber within St Bart's Hospital. Down below us, on an operating table, rested the body of a recently deceased woman.

"This is like cheese to a mouse. Resistance is futile. They are searching for the best in female specimens, so we are giving them one. Besides, we foiled their last attempt when you ignited the creature with the lantern," said Holmes playfully.

"Quite right," I returned. "How do you know they'll read the articles we posted in the papers?"

"Because they scour for information on recent deaths; how else would they know about the graves they were robbing? They are planners, Watson, they don't simply stumble upon something they want, they map out how to get it! Come, let us hide. It will be another long night, but thankfully not as cold and wet." Holmes and I crept along and peered down below, watching and waiting for our trap to be triggered. The room was utterly black, apart from the silver moonlight pouring through the windows above and the few lights that illuminated the halls leading to the upper and lower parts of the chamber. For the longest time, we heard no noise at all, but then, we heard the door to the operating room slowly creak open. I could hear the shuffling of feet across the floor and heavy breathing in and out, almost in a growl. "Let us move slowly, we do not want to be had like last time," Holmes mouthed. "Get your revolver ready."

"It is. Let's go." We stood, keeping ourselves in the shadows, and saw the creature down below. It removed the cover and looked at the dead woman before reaching down and lifting her up over his shoulder. I aimed my revolver at the monster below, but suddenly the door to our left opened, and there in the frame stood a tall, thin man with wild hair, aiming a revolver at us.

"You will not foil my plans again, Mr Holmes!" came the chilled voice of this second, unknown figure.

"I'm not sure we've been introduced," Holmes said calmly.

"Nor shall we," said he. "Creature! Take the body and go!" he yelled.

"Yes," it replied in a deep, monstrous tone and walked out of the operating chamber.

"Now, I wish you no harm. I simply ask that you leave me be," said the man.

"Unfortunately, I cannot do that. Your monster is most certainly responsible for the death of the watchman at Nunhead, and he must be stopped," said Holmes.

"Oh, of course it is responsible, and you can have him soon enough, just not tonight." The man fired his weapon, and we dove out of the way. I tried to pull myself up but felt a sharp pain in my arm.

"Watson! Watson, where are you?" cried Holmes.

"I'm here, Holmes," I called back.

"Are you safe?" He asked me, approaching.

"I've been shot, but it's nothing serious."

"Come, let me get you bandaged up. Thank God you are safe, my friend!" Holmes found some bandages and treated my wound.

"I should have been faster than this," I apologised.

"I am just grateful you are alive. We are dealing with something entirely unbelievable. Something beyond rational science and sanity."

"You are correct, Holmes. But what do we do now? I don't think we'll be able to fool them again."

"He won't get far. I know who he is."

"You do?!" I ejaculated.

"Of course, if you observed, he wore a ring, a ring which bore a family crest belonging to the family called Pretorius. The man we saw tonight was Doctor Septimus Pretorius."

"How could you possibly know this?!"

"Just like you remember what drawer you keep your socks in, I know where to look in my mind to recall useful information," said Holmes with a slight grin. "The Pretorius family has a castle outside the city. We shall go there tonight, but not without speaking to Inspector Bradstreet. It's time we let him in on what we know!"

We found Inspector Bradstreet in his little office at Scotland Yard. We recounted to him the events of the past few days and what we had learnt. "Holmes, I'm surprised at you! Monsters and mad scientists, just pieces of fiction. I suppose you found fairies in the cellar of Baker Street too?" he remarked.

"It is no fiction, Inspector. We've seen the creature. It is most certainly responsible for the death of the watchman," I said sternly.

"Poppycock! It was simply someone dressed up in some kind of performance costume," Bradstreet replied.

"Either way, Inspector, Pretorius and this associate are the ones responsible for the robberies and the murder. I believe they are planning something fiendish and we must stop them!" Holmes pressed.

"Well, you say they are responsible for the murder, so I'll go with you on that, but I am not about to believe some zombie is working with this… Precarious," Bradstreet stammered.

"His name is Pretorius," I corrected.

"Don't matter, they are killers. Give me a bit to rally up some men, and we'll be on our way."

"Very well, Inspector," Holmes conceded.

*****

Soon, Bradstreet, Holmes, I, along with two other officers, were splashing down the cobbled streets of London in a carriage, making our way to the countryside to Pretorius's castle. The night air was heavy as a brewing storm crept in. By the time we were outside the city, a gentle rainfall had begun. Here and there, the sound of thunder rolled in the distance. To our surprise, lightning suddenly filled the sky and spooked the horse. It made a sharp turn, and the back wheel collided with a large rock. The driver was thrown, and we were tossed around inside. The carriage shuddered to a halt as the horse calmed down, and the four of us crawled out, finding one of the other officers in serious pain from a broken leg.

"Well, this is just dandy!" exclaimed Bradstreet.

"Time is precious, Inspector. We must carry on!"

"I have an injured man, Holmes, I must see to that and this broken carriage!" Bradstreet returned.

"I'm sorry, but we must keep going! You do what you need, we'll be at Pretorius's castle," said Holmes, who then tapped me on the arm and walked off.

"Officer Williams, you take the horse and fetch us some aid. I'll stay with Jones until you return. When you get back, we'll meet up with Holmes and Watson at the castle," I heard

Bradstreet instruct as we continued on down the dark path. Holmes and I waded through the drizzling fog as we continued our journey towards the castle.

"What are you expecting to find once we get there?" I asked.

"I am uncertain. We should prepare ourselves for something utterly horrific, though," said Holmes. "Ah, looks like we've arrived." We found ourselves at the long drive leading to the castle. The east tower was the only area lit up, and we could see shadows passing by the windows. Then, in a great explosion, a tremendous bolt of lightning connected with an iron rod extended from the east tower.

"Let us hurry, Watson!" cried Holmes, and we ran towards the main entrance. Holmes picked the lock to the giant front door, and we rushed inside. We ran down corridors until we came to the base of a spiral staircase. The sound of heavy machinery pumping was getting louder, and the shouts of Dr Pretorius echoed down towards us. When we reached the top, there was a circular wall surrounding the laboratory. I peeked through a large keyhole in the door. I saw the creature standing over a figure that appeared to be strapped to a table. It was shaking violently and screeching.

"Ready, Watson?" Holmes asked.

"Wherever you go, Holmes, I follow." With revolvers drawn, we kicked the doorway in. The creature and Dr Pretorius looked at us in shock. I then saw what was strapped to the table, which now stood on one end. It was a woman, or at least the shape of a woman. She was covered from head to toe in wrappings.

"Creatures! Kill them both!" screamed Dr Pretorius. The male creature then pulled a lever down and the bars which restrained the woman were lifted. With her arms free, she tore away the wrapping from her head to reveal the most horrendously beautiful face I had ever seen! There was a crazed, animal-like expression upon this female creature's face as she took in the new world around her. The creatures started moving towards us.

"Another step and we will shoot!" yelled Holmes.

"Pretorius, call them off!" I shouted.

"Attack!" Pretorius ordered as he scrambled for his papers to make good his escape. Holmes fired a shot, and a cylinder above exploded, making the two monsters flinch.

"It's over, Pretorius! Scotland Yard is on their way," yelled Holmes.

"It's only just beginning!" roared Pretorius. Suddenly, I was ambushed! Through the steam, the female creature lunged at me and tackled me to the ground. She wrapped her cold, dead fingers around my neck and began to squeeze. "Holmes! Help!" I choked out. The she-daemon was wide-eyed and drooled at the mouth as she shrieked and continued to strangle me. There was a bang, and she took her hands off me to hold her stomach. I shoved her off and dragged myself away.

"My bride!" yelled the creature.

"My creation!" yelled Pretorius. The male creature turned its pale dead face towards Dr Pretorius, its sunken eyes filled with anger.

"Your… creation?" it said slowly. As they stared at each other, the female creature held her wound, and I rushed to Holmes's side.

"What's going on?" I asked.

"Pretorius called her 'his creation,' and the creature called her his 'bride.' Think of it like two animals staking their claim over one female," whispered Holmes. "Stay here,

242

I'm going to sneak around and close the door behind Pretorius. We cannot let him escape. You lock the one behind me."

"Very well."

"Don't just stand there, you vile insects! Stop the sleuth and the doctor! Bring me their brains! I'll use them to create something truly remarkable!" cried Dr Pretorius.

"We are not insects! We are the Adam and Eve of your labours!" said the creature.

"I am your god! You will obey me!" Dr Pretorius shouted.

"Life… doesn't come… from the dead. Death… is all we know!" uttered the female monster with great effort. Her first words were something utterly profound.

"You are but fallen angels! Daemons! I need you not!" When Dr Pretorius finished, he reached out and pulled a lever which triggered the machinery within the laboratory. Everything was boiling and vibrating. I saw the door behind Pretorius close just as he turned to leave through it. He pulled the handle but it wouldn't move; he shook it violently. Both creatures were slowly walking towards him. I snuck out the door behind me and closed it just as the pipes burst inside the laboratory. I raced around and found Holmes on the other side of the other door. We were listening.

"You should have left me buried in the ice," growled the male creature.

"I wanted to give you life! Give you everything that Frankenstein failed to give you and let the world see what I could do!" Dr Pretorius exclaimed.

"You… want power… you want… to be a god," stammered the woman beast.

"Get us out of here, and you can go free! You can forget me and I'll forget you!" Dr Pretorius pleaded.

"We are creatures born out of death and death is all that comes from us!" roared the male creature. There was a forceful thud against the door as both creatures took Dr Pretorius's life. There was a violent explosion; the laboratory door was blown off, and Holmes and I were thrown back. I looked into the demolished room and saw Dr Pretorius's body on the ground next to the two creatures. As Holmes and I struggled to our feet, we heard a loud crack and observed the floor beginning to give way.

"It is time we get out of here!" Holmes said with haste. We raced down the stairs, through the corridors, and out the front door. From a fair distance away, we turned to see the tower explode. Bricks shot through the air and we dove for cover. "And so ends the horror of Frankenstein," Holmes said gravely once he had composed himself.

*****

A few days later, Holmes and I were sitting in the study of 221b. Holmes was lounging in his chair, smoking, while I sat at the table attempting to compile the events.

"I'm not sure I know where to begin in cataloguing these events," I sighed.

"Perhaps, Watson, there is no need to attempt such an undertaking. The tale would be too extreme for the public to handle. They would assume you had drifted into fantasy instead of accurately retelling events of our cases," Holmes said between puffs.

"That could be true. Inspector Bradstreet even refused to believe our tale in its entirety."

"Bradstreet is quite the fool to believe that I could be tricked by people dressed in theatre costumes! But his reaction, I believe, is only a reflection of what the wider public would assume."

"I suppose the world may never know the horror of Frankenstein."

END

Save Undershaw

In 2009 John Gibson, Lynn Gale, and Sue Meadows joined together and created the Undershaw Preservation Trust, a group devoted to protecting Undershaw, the former home of Sir Arthur Conan Doyle, from redevelopment into townhouses. It was here, in this now *empty house*, where it is said Doyle was at his best. It was in this home, that Doyle himself designed, where he wrote the literary classic 'The Hound of the Baskervilles' and where he brought Sherlock Holmes back to life in 'The Return of Sherlock Holmes.' It was also in this house where he entertained guests such as Bram Stoker, author of Dracula, and J.M. Barrie, author of Peter Pan and more.

The Undershaw Preservation Trust has grown significantly, gaining support not just within the U.K. but around the world. Holmes fans have joined together and signed petitions, wrote letters to Members of Parliament, gave financially, wrote stories, attended the Judicial Review, tweeted, shared and liked the facebook page, and much more with one single purpose, Save Undershaw! Support for Save Undershaw has reached the ears of Mark Gatiss, writer for the incredibly successful BBC Sherlock, who acts as patron for this project, as well as Stephen Fry who agree that the destruction of this estate would be a great shame. Sir Arthur Conan Doyle has given the world not only two of the most beloved characters in Sherlock Holmes & Doctor Watson but also given the world many other great stories and novels like the dinosaur epic The Lost World and other haunting tales.

The Undershaw Preservation Trust needs your help and support. Though they have won the May 2012 Judicial Review there is still a long road ahead. Undershaw is not out of the woods yet. Take part in history and help us Save Undershaw. Find them on Facebook and help raise awareness of this mission. The Undershaw Preservation Trust needs your help to raise funds. Two ways of doing so are 1) popping over to their website and pledging 2) picking up a copy of *Sherlock's Holmes & The Case of the Crystal Blue Bottle: A Graphic Novel*. What better way to support than to pick up a brand new story about Sherlock Holmes! All proceeds from *Crystal Blue Bottle* go to support Undershaw and to help its development.

To find out more and to show support for The Undershaw Preservation Trust follow these links.

Website: http://www.saveundershaw.com/

Facebook: https://www.facebook.com/saveundershaw

Twitter: https://twitter.com/#!/Save_Undershaw

More From Luke Kuhns

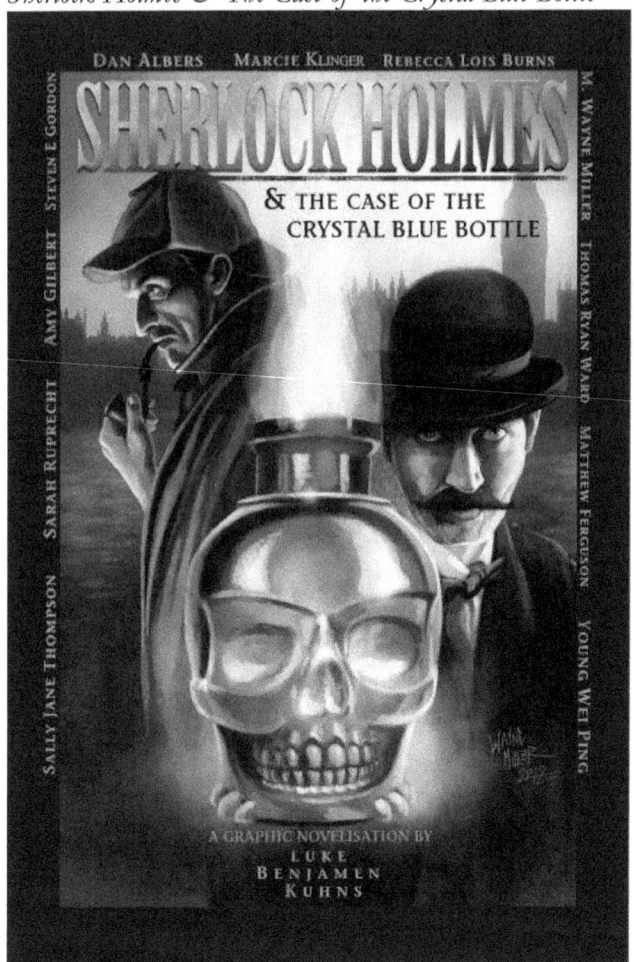

Artwork from

Sherlock Holmes & The Case of the Crystal Blue Bottle

Steven E Gordon

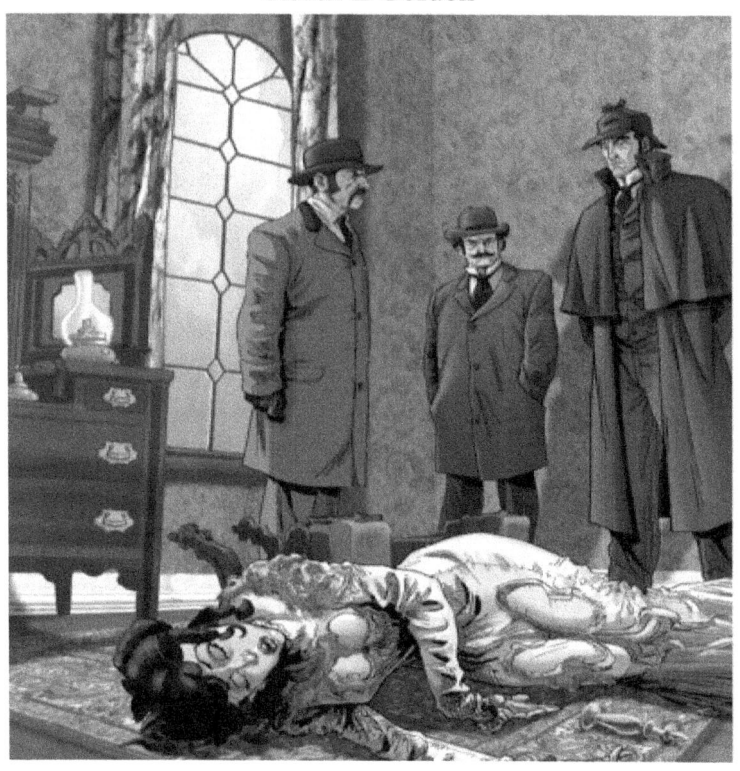

Sherlock Holmes & The Case of the Crystal Blue Bottle: A Graphic Novel. This story first appeared in the 2012 *Sherlock's Home: The Empty House*, a book written by Holmes fans and authors from around the world, with contributions from Mark Gatiss & Stephen Fry. With 11 illustrators from Singapore, America, the UK, and Europe wishing to support Undershaw, Crystal Blue Bottle was transformed into a beautiful graphic novel featuring stunning artwork from some of the industry's finest. Contributors include Steven E Gordon (The Great Mouse Detective, X-Men Evolution, Lord of the Rings), Matthew Ferguson (Marvel's The Avengers & Star Wars), Wayne Miller, Marcie Klinger, Sarah Ruprecht, and more. This is a great book to add to your Holmes collection.

Other titles
The Scarlet Thread of Murder

Sherlock Holmes and the Horror of Frankenstein

Welcome to Undershaw

www.ingramcontent.com/pod-product-compliance
Lightning Source LLC
Chambersburg PA
CBHW071136260626
47162CB00003B/804